DINNER FOR TWO
TIMES TWO
TIMES TWO . . .

"Wait a moment. Every time it feeds it takes on a new form, that right?"

"Presumably," Tom agreed.

"And the new form is—is twins?"

"Well, that would explain everything very neatly, wouldn't it?"

Suddenly Dr. Innis jumped to his feet, the horrifying truth of the situation now chillingly clear. "If it can absorb the power of speech and rational thought along with the shape of the human body, then after a few more feeds the creatures are going to be fully equipped with everything they need—language, comprehension, everything—to pass themselves off as . . . as members of our own species . . ."

DOUBLE, DOUBLE

John Brunner

A Del Rey Book

BALLANTINE BOOKS • NEW YORK

A Del Rey Book
Published by Ballantine Books

ISBN 0-345-27964-6

Manufactured in the United States of America

First Edition: January 1969
Second Printing: January 1979

Cover art by Murray Tinkelman

DOUBLE, DOUBLE

I

COMING TOWARD YOU it looked as though a piano with hydrophobia had suddenly run wild and opened huge bulbous eyes like a frog's but with enormous thick—somehow sad—lashes. The white and black keyboard of fangs was painted on the radiator grille, the lashes surrounded the headlights. Splaying out along the sides were Art Nouveau curlicues forming frames the size and shape of double crown posters—green, orange, brown, purple. The poster-sized frames were filled with posters, gaudier and more complex than the designs swirling around them. All of them said, somewhere among their fat bulges and curves: BRUNO AND THE HERMETIC TRADITION. Sitting on the roof, dangling its lax tentacles three to a side and one each to front and rear, was an inflatable rubber octopus that had a tire valve under the middle left-hand tentacle. Whenever they had the tires of the van checked, they always said, "And—uh—blow up the octopus, will you? We have eighteen pounds in that."

It had been a regular Ford Transit, delivered from the factory in sober dark green. That, though, was way, back. The changes didn't stop with the paint job—the whole interior had been made over, with bunks and Lilo mattresses and boxes to hold the instruments and amplifiers, and a radio and a record player and . . .

But it was the paint job, of course, that made people feel it wasn't what you'd expect to see coming down a quiet English country lane. Once this trip a nervous old

7

lady had practically climbed into a hedgerow before she realized she wasn't being charged by a four-wheeled dragon.

"Ah, hell," said Bruno Twentyman, and put on the brakes. "Looks like we've run out of road again."

Lounging in the rear of the van, using Nancy Lane's back as a lectern for the copy of *Evergreen Review* he was reading, Gideon Hard said without raising his dark-brown head, "Man, I *told* you that last signpost pointed to 'Bringdown.' "

"Gid, we heard you the first time and it wasn't any funnier then!" Looking harassed, Bruno ran his short thick capable fingers comb-fashion through his shock of frizzy dark hair. Ahead, the potholed lane they were following was cut off by a gate with a sign hung on it; beyond, there was only a grassy field seamed with a rutted track that dived out of sight behind a knoll, and the sea, calm now in the evening sunshine after the wind and rain of the early afternoon.

For the dozenth time he added, "Glenn, are you *sure* about this place we're looking for?"

"Shit, man, I keep telling you," Glenn Salmon said in an aggrieved tone. "I saw it from the deck of the Antwerp boat—chalk cliffs and a little beach in between, clean as a cheese with a wedge cut out!" His voice climbed from its normal, rather lazy Midwestern drawl toward the high nasal Ozark whine of his grandparents. "Hell, it must be somewhere around here! There's chalk all over these fields, like someone spilled a bag of flour on them!"

"Sure, but it doesn't seem to go anywhere near the water," Bruno grunted. "And all we've found is mud flats, not beaches. Cress, light me a cigarette, will you?"

Jammed in the middle of the front seat between him

8

and the pudgy bulk of the American, Cressida Beggarstaff wriggled to comply.

"Mind that hipbone, baby!" Glenn winced. "I thought it was a great idea your coming in the front because you're the thinnest. But you're *lumpy*."

Elf-slim in brilliant blue bellbottoms and a Paisley shirt, Cress gave him a sidelong scowl under her mass of fair hair.

"Afraid I'll burst you and let all the hot air out? Here, Bruno—your cigarette."

"What does the sign on that gate say?" Liz Howell demanded from the back of the van, in the tone of some-one changing the subject to prevent a row breaking out. "Can't quite see from here."

"Want the binoculars?" Glenn suggested sourly. But he made no move to take them from the ledge above the dashboard where they were lying.

"It says 'Ministry of Agriculture and Fisheries, Brin-down Research Station,'" Bruno read out. "Not that that leaves me any the wiser. . . . So what do I do now, Glenn? You're in charge."

The American hesitated, glancing at the map of Kent spread out on his knees. He took his glasses off, gave them a rapid rub with a buttercup-yellow handkerchief, and returned them to his broad-bridged nose. After a pause he said, "Gid, are you sure this place I saw couldn't be anywhere else?"

"Oh, for—!" The West Indian shut his magazine with a slap and eeled around to reach over Glenn's shoulder with one forefinger extended like a dagger. "Baby, you saw me figure out the distance on the geological map! You said you spotted this chalk cliff from the Antwerp boat at 7:15 A.M. That means you must have been between *here* and *here*." He jabbed at the map so hard the paper nearly tore. "This is the only bit of North Kent where the chalk runs clear to the sea. Go any further east and you run out of chalk altogether until you get past the North Foreland. *I* think you were dreaming of the White Cliffs of Dover—couldn't bear to miss them on your first trip to this country."

"Put a stopper in it, Gid," Bruno said wearily. "But the fact remains, Glenn: we've taken every bloody road we can find around here, and we've come up with"—he ticked them off on his fingers—"one caravan site, one Roman ruin, some crazy kind of chemical factory, and this. Whatever it is."

"It's getting late!" Nancy Lane said with a toss of her sleek dark head. "What time is it, anyway?"

"About eight, I think," Cress said, and glanced at her watch. "Yes, just gone five to."

"Well, we can go on for a while yet," Glenn said. "The sun will be up for at least another hour."

"But I'm getting hungry," Nancy complained. It was clear she was having trouble stopping herself from losing her temper. Her round, pretty face was carved with deep furrows, either side of her mouth.

"Dip in the lunch-basket," Gideon suggested, unfolding himself back along the bunk where he had stretched out before.

"Lunch-basket!" Nancy burst out. "Marvellous picnic we had today, didn't we? Bucketing down with rain—"

"You're going to hold me responsible for the goddamned weather now?" Glenn snapped, twisting around to glare at her.

"I don't mind going on for a bit," Liz offered. "It's turned out fine now, hasn't it? And this is a part of the country I haven't seen before."

"Yes, but—" Bruno hesitated, flipping his ash out of the open window beside him. "I'm wondering if there's much point. You may not be able to get to this beach

Glenn saw, from the landward side. I mean there may not be a road leading to it. In which case it won't be much good to us, will it?"

"Not unless we hire a steamer and bring people to it by water," Cress said.

Glenn brightened. "Say, wouldn't that be a great gimmick? We could tie it in with *Seadeath* and maybe get a trained dolphin to make like Pelorus Jack and—"

"Glenn, it's complicated enough the way it is," Bruno sighed. "I told you all along: it's a terrific idea. But unless we can get coachloads of people to the place, it's out—*punkt*."

"Okay okay *okay*!" Glenn slapped the map shut. "Let's call the whole deal off, hm? Let's go feed Nancy like she wants us to."

"Maybe we could hire a boat tomorrow and look it over from the sea?" Nancy said apologetically.

"No, forget it, forget it!" Glenn shoved the map, roughly folded, under the binoculars and tugged a cigarette from the breast pocket of his green and gold shirt. "It was probably a stupid idea in the first place."

There was a depressed silence. Gideon broke it by stretching as far as the confines of the van allowed. "Know something?" he said. "I think we've all spent too much of this fine evening cooped up inside here. Let's at least get out and walk around a bit before we head for home."

"Yes, grandpa," Cress murmured. Gideon made a face at her. But the fact that he was ten years older than anyone else in the group had become a sort of family joke, and there was no malice in it.

"Look, there's someone coming," Liz said, pointing past Bruno's shoulder. Glancing up, the others saw a man in his early thirties, wearing a faded blue shirt and gray slacks, trudging across the thick grass of the field beside the sea. "Maybe we could ask him if he knows the place Glenn means."

"Good thought," Bruno said, switching off the engine and opening his door. Instantly, there was a rushing movement through the grass and a huge brown dog dived under the fence and hurled itself upon him, wuffing with delight, tail going nineteen to the dozen, almost bowling him over with excitement.

II

CONSIDERING THE RAIN had been over since three and the evening had turned out fine and warm, Tom Reedwall was in a bad mood.

"That damnable dog," he said under his breath. "Where in the—?"

He broke off, thinking he had spotted the ball he was looking for, but it was only a lump of bare earth of roughly the same reddish-brown color as the rubber. Ahead, behind, and all around, Inkosi yapped joyously, pleased at his own ability to make his master look foolish.

"That'll be the third one you've lost in a fortnight if you don't find it," Tom told him sternly. "Come on, fetch it, *fetch* it! Oh, blast—now what is it?"

Without warning the dog had wheeled and started to race inland, away from the crumbling cliff-steep banks of clay that here marked the edge of the sea. Only a line of disturbed grass crests showed the direction he was taking. He was not yet full-grown, and—judging by the way he was behaving at the moment—even when he was, he was likely to retain a good many puppyish characteristics.

Sighing, Tom raised his head, and started as he caught sight of what had attracted Inkosi's attention. A van, done over in such a phantasmagoria of different colors that it was practically camouflaged against the hedgerows at the end of the lane leading to the main road, had pulled up in front of the gate marking the boundary of the research station's territory. As the driver got out—a man in his early twenties wearing a sort of windbreaker in vivid red and white stripes—Inkosi jumped up at him, tongue flapping like a limp pink rag.

Hampered by the dense grass, still wet from the earlier rain, Tom hurried toward the van to apologize. As he approached, others got out to join the driver: a plump man with glasses in a brilliant green and gold shirt, a fair girl in bellbottom trousers, then two more girls, both very pretty and wearing minidresses, one fair, one dark, and finally a tall, lean colored man, rather older than his companions, in a knitted cotton sweater and lime-green slacks.

Luckily, Tom realized, they didn't seem put out by the dog's assault; all, except the man with glasses, were grinning and making a fuss of him. As he reached the gate, the girl in bellbottoms called to him.

"Is he yours?"

"That's right," Tom called back.

"He's lovely! What's his name? And what *is* he?"

"He's a Ridgeback," Tom said, leaning on the gate and folding his arms. "And we call him Inkosi. That's Zulu for 'chieftain.'"

"Inkosi!" the girl said. The dog slapped his tail back and forth like an oar and woofed with pleasure, the skin under his spinal ridge of reversed hairs wriggling like the surface of a stormy sea. There was a pause.

"Ah—are you looking for a way down to the water?" Tom suggested eventually, prepared to explain why they couldn't get through this way.

"Sort of," said the man with glasses in an American accent. "Say, do you happen to know a beach near here with chalk cliffs overhanging it?"

Taken aback, Tom hesitated, and the man amplified his question. "You see, I spotted a place from the deck of the boat that brought me over from Antwerp, and I brought my friends down here hunting it because Gideon"—a nod at the colored man—"says this is where it must be. But we've been looking all afternoon without finding it."

"It's got to be around here somewhere, I guess," Gideon said. "I checked with a geological map. This is the last bit of chalk for miles."

"Well, that's quite right, in fact," Tom confirmed. "But I think you've come too far east."

"I don't see how we can have," the American objected. "We tried every other road we could find, and the last place we got to looked like some kind of chemical factory, with nothing around it but mud banks."

"That'll be the Organic Acids depot," Tom said, and gave a scowl against his will.

"You don't like 'em, hm?" suggested Gideon.

"Well—ah—no, frankly, I don't," Tom agreed. "They give us a lot of trouble here. Pollution. They don't monitor their effluents properly."

"You work at this research station?" the man in the striped windbreaker inquired.

"That's right. I'm Dr. Tom Reedwall."

"We're Bruno and the Hermetic Tradition—or rather, the majority of it." The man in the windbreaker gave an embarrassed grin. "It's a joke of Gideon's. I'm Bruno—Bruno Twentyman."

The colored man shrugged. "Ran across it in *The New York Review of Books,*" he said. "I saw where someone had written a book called *Giordano Bruno and the Hermetic Tradition,* and I thought that was a hell of a name for a pop group. We were looking for a name at the time—just getting started."

Tom straightened, snapping his fingers. "Haven't I been hearing a record of yours on the radio lately?" he demanded.

Bruno grimaced. "Could be—we had a single that

made the Top Twenty about a month back. In at number twenty one week, out at number twenty the next."

"Wasn't it something about the skin diver who met a dolphin?" Tom said, frowning with the effort of recollection.

"Right. *Seadeath*, we called it. Gid here wrote the words and Glenn"—he nodded at the American—"and our missing member, Rupert White, did the music."

Gideon sang gently:

> *"And the shells were yellow and the shells were red*
> *But the sea was redder when I shot him dead*
> *And he sank to the ocean's bed—bed—b-e-ed!"*

He peaked on a shrill falsetto which, on the record, had been the signal for a sudden tremulous echo effect; then he broke off with a smile, pulling a pack of cigarettes from his pocket and offering them to Tom. "I'm Gideon Hard, by the way. And this is Cress—and Nancy—and Liz."

Tom declined the cigarette, but produced his charred old pipe and began to fill it. Inkosi, exhausted, had slumped down on the ground at Cress's feet, and she had dropped on one knee to continue scratching his ears.

"You haven't any dolphins here, have you?" demanded the girl who had been introduced as Liz, the fair one in the minidress—eye-searing black, blue, and red.

Tom chuckled and shook his head. "Not at the moment, no. They like warmer water than this. But as it happens, we are hoping to get some. We've been building a specially heated pen recently. . . . It's not our speciality, though. We're chiefly interested in fish as food—trying to turn fishermen from hunters to farmers, you might say."

"So where do the dolphins come in?" Cress looked up from her fondling of Inkosi. "They aren't even fish, are they?"

16

"Quite right—they're mammals. But eventually it might be possible to train them like sheepdogs, to herd shoals of fish for us."

"Sounds like you have a—well, a professional interest in that song of mine," Gideon said.

Tom shrugged. "Not exactly, though I suppose that's why it caught my attention. To be perfectly frank, I don't think I ever listened to it all the way through. Just happened to hear it because someone had the radio going. It was about this diver who found a dolphin making patterns of colored shells on the seabed, right?"

"And shot him with a harpoon-gun," Gideon nodded.

"What for?"

"Man, you tell me! But isn't it the truth? If this here dolphin had come at him shooting, like with a bow and arrows, the cat would have said *intelligent* and *civilized*, even! But he finds this beastie making pretty patterns with shells and weed, and—pow!" Gideon pantomimed firing a gun.

"A symbol of the way we treat artists and poets in our culture," Bruno said.

"That's too deep for me," Gideon said. "I meant it to mean just exactly what it said."

"When correctly viewed, everything is lewd," Glenn quoted with a gesture of dismissal. "Don't start that argument up again, for Chrissake. Like, it's a pretty song and it doesn't need footnotes."

Tom pushed himself back to an upright stance, snapping his fingers at Inkosi.

"Well, I'd better be getting home," he said. "I was just taking the dog for a walk before supper."

"One moment," Glenn said hastily. "*Do* you know this place with the chalk cliff?"

"Ah—yes, I think I do know a spot like that." Tom

17

hesitated. "A little narrow triangle of beach, the cliffs not very high, about twenty or thirty feet?"

"That sounds exactly like it," Glenn confirmed.

"Glenn thinks it would be the perfect site for an open-air freakout," Bruno said.

Tom shook his head. "I don't think I quite get you."

"A big session running maybe all night with music and dancing and a barbecue on the beach and all kinds of colored slides and films projected on the white chalk," Bruno explained. "But if you can't get to it from the road, there's not much point in looking for the place. On the night, we'd have to deliver coachloads of people, you see."

"If the place I'm thinking of is the same one," Tom said thoughtfully, "there's no road leading directly to it, but there's a lane that runs within maybe a hundred yards. It's about halfway between Brindown and Geddesley. There's a little copse with a gate alongside. But I don't know who the land belongs to, I'm afraid. They might not want people dancing on the beach."

"Well, that's always something that has to be sorted out," Bruno said. "But thanks very much anyway. We'll have one last go at finding it before we go home, then. In spite of you being so hungry, Nancy!"

The dark-haired girl shrugged. "I'll do what Gideon suggested—take a nosh out of the lunch-basket."

"We were going to have a picnic, you see," Bruno said. "Only it was pelting down with rain at lunch-time. . . . Well, never mind. We found quite a nice pub and had some sandwiches instead. Right, shall we blow?"

Nodding and smiling farewells to Tom, they began to climb back into the decorated van. Tom whistled Inkosi to his feet and began to head for home. It wasn't until he was indoors that he remembered the ball he had thrown, which the dog had failed to bring back.

III

"WELL, WELL, WELL—the prodigal returns!" Netta Reedwall put her pretty head around the kitchen door and blew a kiss to her husband. At first reluctant to come back indoors, Inkosi suddenly sniffed the scent of cooking that wafted toward him, and charged head-down to see if there was anything in his food-bowl. Finding there wasn't, he gave a sort of canine shrug and folded himself away in a corner.

"Yes, sorry to have been so long." Tom picked up the glass he had left when he had taken the dog out, and bent to the drinks cabinet. "First that ruddy animal lost his ball, and I'm afraid I didn't manage to locate it either. Then I met some very interesting young people at the end of the drive. . . . Have I time for another one before we eat?"

"I should think so, provided you include me in. Here!" Netta emerged from the kitchen, an apron over her trim flower-printed summer frock, holding out her own glass. Taking it, Tom stared at her so hard she became uncomfortable.

"Something wrong?" she demanded at last.

"No, nothing. I was just thinking nobody would ever suspect you of having a biology degree."

"You old flatterer. But I love you for it." Netta dropped into a chair, facing him. "So who were these people you met?"

"Remember that song about a skin diver who met a

19

dolphin, which they played on the radio a lot recently? I met the group who recorded it, with their girl-friends, in the most extraordinary van you ever saw—painted like a jungle run riot."

"What on earth were they doing here?" Netta said. "And were they nice?"

"Oh, they seemed very pleasant. They were looking for a bit of beach with chalk cliffs around it, to hold an all-night freakout, they said."

"Oh, that sounds like fun!" Netta exclaimed. "Could we go?"

"Don't see why not." Tom handed her the drink he had mixed. "Though I doubt if they'll be able to arrange it. The only bit of ground I could call to mind that matched what they described was that piece west of here where the extraordinary old woman lives all by herself in the burnt-out house—know what I mean?"

"Oh, yes! Miss . . ." Netta hesitated. "Miss Beeding, is that her name?"

"Something like that," Tom agreed. "I've no idea whether she actually owns the land, but I suppose she must do—otherwise she probably wouldn't be allowed to live there." He plumped into his own chair with a sigh. "I rather hope they do manage to fix it, though—it'd make for a bit of light relief around here, and I need some!"

"You had a bad day, did you?" Netta said sympathetically. "I meant to ask."

"I wish I was a beautiful girl like you," Tom muttered. "All you need do is wiggle your hips at the boss, and he melts like a jellyfish stranded on a rock and caves in. Me, I have to argue, and Doc Innis isn't so susceptible to logic."

"Darling, he's not the trouble—let's face it!" Netta leaned forward. "The trouble around here goes by the name of Sam Fletcher, and if you accuse me of wiggling my hips at him, I'll—I'll throw my drink at you! I don't *have* to! In fact I have to try not to!"

"Has that bastard been bothering you again?" Tom snapped.

"Oh—no worse than usual, I suppose. And probably he can't help it. He's such a slimy person he probably can't get a girl of his own."

Tom rose restlessly from his chair and walked to the window overlooking the little bay in which the research station was sited. Their bungalow had originally been intended for a caretaker, rather than members of the research staff, but some economically minded official in the Ministry of Agriculture and Fisheries had noted that there was a joint application from husband and wife to fill the two vacancies resulting from recent promotions, and had seen a way to save subsidizing the rents of the new employees. He had no particular objection on that score— free accommodation meant that the salary from the job was worth much more than he'd expected—but it did make their evenings rather lonely, being stranded here on the edge of the sea. Besides, the bungalow was too cramped for them to do as they had planned and start a family; there was no spare room for a child. That would have to wait until he received his next pay increment a year from now.

However, it was certainly a very pleasant situation, and the view was fine—clear across the arm of the sea which, a few miles to the west, turned into the estuary of the Thames. Closer, there were the low-roofed buildings that formed the research station: labs, fish-ponds, administrative offices, and the latest acquisition, which he had mentioned to Bruno and his companions—the pens where eventually it was hoped to install at least a pair of dolphins for training as fish-herds. At present they were still rather a mess; not even the heavy rain of midday had washed away the cleated tracks of the contractors' vehicles. But given a month or two to scatter a bit of grass seed over the surrounding soil, they would blend in nicely with the rest of the layout.

Down at the wharf, the station's little launch rocked in the wake of a freighter passing toward Port of London. He watched it moodily, taking another sip from his drink.

"Has there been any more news about the plane crash?" Netta said from behind him.

"What? Oh, sorry, I was dreaming." He turned to her. "You mean the one that went down in the sea the other day? No, I think they gave up trying to recover the wreckage. There was no hope for the pilot, anyway."

Netta shuddered. "It must have been an awful death," she said. "I mean, if he lived through the actual crash. Imagine being trapped in the cockpit of a plane under the sea, knowing that you couldn't live longer than the oxygen lasted."

"He might have tried to get out and swim to the surface," Tom shrugged. "And drowning is supposed to be quite a pleasant way to die, isn't it?"

"Don't be so morbid!"

There was a melancholy silence while they both thought of the past few days' events: the crash of a plane during an experimental test flight; then the arrival of police launches and a naval tug with trawls and dredges, trying to locate it, all of which had at one time or another put in at the research station's tiny wharf alongside their own launch, which was named after the codfish, *Morrhua*.

At length Netta sighed and emptied her glass, setting it down with a clink. "Supper should be ready now," she said. "I wonder how your friends are making out in their search for a site."

"A copse with a gate beside it," Bruno said, and slowed

down. "Do you suppose that could be what the guy meant?"

"It looks promising," Cress agreed.

"Right, we'll reconnoiter," Bruno said. "Just let me go on a bit and find a place where I can pull off the road."

At walking pace they passed the gate he had spotted, and all of them—even Gideon, who normally affected a blasé pose—peered out through the side and rear windows.

"There's chalk here all right!" Glenn exclaimed, pointing at a patch of bare earth exposed alongside the roots of a tree.

"Don't get too worked up," Bruno counseled. "Ah, here's a spot where we can leave the van. It'll be bumpy— hold on!"

He ran the van half off the edge of the narrow road, with its wheels resting on a steep grassy verge, and switched off the engine.

"Foof! Isn't it hot?" Nancy exclaimed.

"Always complaining about something," Gideon murmured. "Too hot, too cold, too hungry, too—"

"Gid, for heaven's sake!" Liz cut in, and the West Indian gave Nancy an affectionate pat on the shoulder.

"Sorry, baby—just a joke in bad taste. You're quite right, it has turned warm this evening. Quite like home, believe me!"

"Anyway, girls have the edge in warm weather," Glenn said as he got out, awkwardly because of the van's closeness to the hedge paralleling the road. "I'll bet I'm having to wear clothes that weigh twice as much as what any of these three have got on."

"I'd like to see you in a miniskirt in the middle of winter," Cress countered as she followed him.

"I wouldn't," Bruno said. "Can't you imagine Glenn's legs—all patchy, blue and red and white?" He shuddered dramatically and led the way across the road. "Hmm! This gate's padlocked!"

"So we climb over," Gideon said, and did so, turning to help the girls scramble after him.

On the other side they found themselves in a field not unlike the one by the research station, but with many more thistles, so that the going was uncomfortable while they crossed it; they were all wearing sandals except Bruno, who had been driving. They forgot that, however, when they had gone the hundred yards or so that Tom Reed-wall mentioned, for they arrived at the brink of exactly the kind of miniature bay Glenn had promised: a wedge of beach, with some comparatively clean sand on the land-ward side despite the fact that farther out it blended into the inevitable mud flats of this area, several large flat rocks apparently isolated from the shore, and irregular walls of pale chalk on either side about twenty-five feet high.

"That's fab," Liz said finally.

"What did I tell you?" Glenn crowed, and strode off around the edge of the inlet to look for a way down. Shortly he found one: a ramplike path, much overgrown with grass and weeds, but still usable, as he proceeded to prove by going down it.

"What do you think?" Gideon said quietly to Bruno. In the six months they had known the American, they had learned to accept his fitful enthusiasms and grown prepared to discount them if they had to.

"I think it could be made to work," Bruno said after a moment's reflection. "We'd have to hire a couple of boats, probably, to put projectors and things on, and I'm not sure about running both a barbecue and dancing on that kind of space, but apart from that, yes, it could work fine."

"We'd have to run some kind of food and drink arrangements," Cress said. "Maybe we could lay on a hot-dog van?"

"And how about the tides?" Gideon added. "It'd be just too goddamned silly if the night we fixed it for proved to be the night the beach was under water!"

"We can check on that, surely," Bruno said. "But you're right, of course. Around here I think the tides do run pretty high."

Having made his way right down to the beach and run around it once, Glenn had now returned to a point directly below them.

"Hey!" he called. "I've had the greatest idea!"

"Not another," Gideon said with a mock groan, and put his head in his hands.

"Shut up, you ignorant Trini-daddy! Listen, Bruno baby, why don't we have our picnic after all? Let's go find a pub and buy some beer or something, and come back and eat what was going to be our lunch. Liz put some terrific food in that basket and it'd be a shame to waste it."

"That sounds marvelous!" Nancy exclaimed.

"Anybody else in favor?" Glenn demanded. When the rest of them shrugged and nodded, he clambered up to rejoin them. "We can sort of make it a dry run for the big event," he said as he reached the head of the path.

"With one transistor radio?" Gideon said. "You must be joking. How do we get sixty watts' amplification out of that?" On seeing Glenn begin to scowl, he added, "Okay— skip it. Yeah, I think it could be kind of fun."

"If it doesn't rain," Bruno said.

"It's a clear sky, baby!" Glenn said, and started back to the van.

IV

THE SUN WAS setting when they came back from locating the pub, because as usual Glenn had suggested having a drink while they were there, and when they finally relocated the place where they had been before they had to stagger across the field, loaded with bottles and the enormous lunch-basket Liz had filled for six people, in that difficult, dim light between day and night when the rods and cones of the retina are uncertain about the changeover of priorities.

But they had almost made it to the edge of the cliff when a voice said sternly out of nowhere, "What are *you* doing?"

They stopped dead, staring at the point from which the voice seemed to come; it was a querulous noise, partway between male and female, ideally matched to the twilight.

"Well?" the voice demanded, and the speaker came into plain sight. As they managed to focus their eyes, they made out an elderly woman, her skirt dragging around her broken-down shoes, her hair apparently gray—though the neutral dusk made it hard to tell—clutching a large, tattered straw bag.

For a long moment they all stood uncertainly wavering. Then Bruno recovered his presence of mind and walked up to her, putting on at maximum force the upper-class air he was generally trying to live down.

"I do beg your pardon if we've inconvenienced you in any way, madam!" he exclaimed. "But my friends and I were just looking for a place to have a night picnic, and that little piece of beach over there—well, it seems like an ideal site. But of course if we're trespassing . . . ?"

He let the end of the sentence hang on the air, so that it seemed to curl into the shape of a question mark.

The old woman sniffed loudly and gave him a searching stare from head to toe.

"A picnic?" she echoed after a pause. And repeated, on a more thoughtful note: "A picnic! Well, well, I didn't know that young people like you went in for such innocent pleasures these days! All this frantic running around, all these cars and airplanes and speedboats and these awful things one reads about in the newspapers!"

Bruno looked as shocked as he could contrive. He said in a tone that was a parody of self-righteousness, "I do *so* much agree. Isn't it terrible, some of the things you see in the papers?"

He beamed at her. After a moment, he added, "Is this land yours, by the way, madam? We would of course have asked permission to come on to it if we'd known who to get in touch with."

"Well, actually . . ." The old woman's face fell. "Actually *no*— I wish it were!" Her tone sounded like a ghastly exaggeration of coquetry, as though in the presence of people half a century her junior she had slipped back to what had passed for sophistication when she had been their age. "But I do live here, you see. Over that way, there's my house."

She pointed, and, turning, they saw the outline of a roof against the darkening sky, with a bite out of it as though some colossal animal had sampled the taste.

"There was a fire, you see," the old woman said. "So I'm afraid I can't possibly invite you in for a cup of tea or anything . . ."

"That's *quite* all right," Bruno said warmly.

"A picnic! Well, well!" She turned back on the original subject. "Yes, what fun that used to be. Maybe now the warmer weather is here I can get about more. . . . However, never mind that. I should introduce myself, should I not? Since there is no mutual acquaintance to—ah—*do the office*, in the phrase I heard from my late friend Captain Horder!" She giggled. "I am Miss Felicia Beeding."

"We're delighted to make your acquaintance," Bruno said solemnly. "I am Bruno Twentyman. Allow me to present Miss Lane, Miss Howell, Miss Beggarstaff, Mr. Salmon, and Mr. Hard."

Miss Beeding gave Gideon a suspicious look and sniffed. "The—ah—the *colonial* person is a friend of yours also?" she said.

"Of course," Bruno said, signaling to Gideon to keep his mouth shut. "Mr. Hard is a British citizen, and to my mind this *far* transcends more superficial considerations."

"Yes, I suppose you're right," Miss Beeding sighed. "Although in my young days . . . Never mind that, however! Ah—you did say a *picnic*, didn't you?"

"Yes."

"Would you by any chance have any—ah—*alcoholic refreshment* for your picnic?"

There was a moment's silence. Finally Bruno said, "Well, we did buy some beer, yes."

"Would it be *too* much to ask if you could spare me a little? It would save me going all the way to the—ah—the establishment which I'm bound for." Pathetic eagerness colored the unsexed voice.

"Certainly," Bruno said. "Liz, pass me one of those bottles, will you?"

"You're so kind!" Miss Beeding was almost dancing on her toes now. "Ah—I'm afraid I'm in rather *straitened circumstances*. . . ."

"Madam, we wouldn't think of asking for payment," Bruno said sternly. "Consider it a gift in reciprocation for your kindness in allowing us to have our picnic here. Please!" He thrust the bottle into her greedy hands.

"Thank you *so* much," she gabbled, and on the point of turning to go, she concluded, "It's very refreshing, I must say, to know that some young people at least have not forgotten the proper way to treat a lady!"

When she had disappeared, and the only hint of her presence was a guggling sound as the beer left the bottle she had been given, Gideon let out a hiss of breath.

"Colonial, hm?" he said with a wealth of overtones.

"Oh, don't worry about her," Cress said. "She's only a poor old dear who's gone a bit batty, isn't she? You were wonderful, Bruno."

"Right," Glenn agreed. "This upper-crust English bit is fantastic. And if she's the only problem we have to contend with if we want to hold a freakout here, we can buy her off with a fifth of whiskey, I guess!"

Liz was staring in the direction of the house with its broken-backed roof. She said at length, "There's hardly anything left of that building, you know. She must be practically camping out in it."

"Smelled like it," Nancy muttered. "Oh, come on! I want to get at that food—it's been ages!"

Cress had brought a flashlight from the van, but when she tried it, going down the path to the beach, she found it was not yet dark enough to be worthwhile. Awkwardly, with some missteps, they managed to follow her without dropping any of the load they were carrying.

"Have to clear that path a bit," Bruno said, heading for a flat, clean patch of sand with a convenient rock they could use as a table. "Got the radio, Nance? Put it on and let's have some music. You ought to be able to pick up Radio Jolly Roger from here—that's lying off Margate, isn't it?"

"Let's get a fire going," Glenn suggested. "Gid, come and find some driftwood."

"It'll probably be soaking wet and smoke like hell," Gideon prophesied gloomily, but he complied. By the time he and Glenn had returned with arms full of wood and clumps of dry grass which had been sheltered by the over-hang of the cliffs from the earlier rain, the girls had set out the contents of the food-basket and the cheerful clamor of the evening pop request show from the nearby pirate radio ship was echoing from the chalk walls.

As Gideon had feared, the wood was wet, but three attempts produced a small, bright blaze around which they could stack the rest of their fuel to dry off before being piled on the fire itself. Luckily, the breeze that had sprung up swirled around the little bay and carried the smoke away from where they were sitting.

"This is fab!" Nancy said around a mouthful of bread and cold chicken. "Sorry for bitching so much, Glenn. This makes up for everything."

Bruno peeled off his windbreaker and reached for a bottle of beer. He took a healthy swig and set it down firmly in the sand to keep it from toppling over.

"It has turned warm, hasn't it?" he said. "It'd be great to have a fine hot night like this for the big event."

"You think it's a deal?" Glenn asked.

"Sure, provided we don't run into any local objections. I mean, it's all very well to talk about buying the old lady off with a bottle. But she said this isn't her land. And even if it's common-land, not part of somebody's farm or some-thing, there'll be some sort of local council, maybe, that we'd have to make arrangements with. And you know how the squares react to this kind of thing."

"We'll have to talk to Monty," Gideon said, referring to the band's agent. "He's bound to be able to sort it out for us."

"I hope you're right," Glenn muttered, and reached for a wedge of cheese from the basket.

In twenty minutes or so the food was almost gone, but there was still plenty of beer. Taking another drink, Bruno leaned contentedly back against the rock they were using for a table and watched as Gideon carefully sorted out the driest of the wood and added it to the fire.

In the now almost total darkness, bar the high faint summer sky-gleam speckled with the brightest stars, he saw the lights of a ship working toward the North Sea. The radio went over to a hair-tonic commercial. Liz, who was nearest, hit the switch, and he spoke into the sudden silence.

"It's a bloody unjust world, isn't it?"

"What makes you say that out of nowhere?" Glenn demanded, passing cigarettes to the girls.

"I was thinking about the old woman—you know, brought up to be a lady, talking about her 'dear friend the captain' and all the rest of it." Bruno took out a cigarette for himself, watching the ship's lights thoughtfully. "And look at the way she's wound up—dirty, shabby, begging for a drink!"

"Being a lady is not enough," Cress said.

"Of course it isn't. But do you think she ever had the chance to make herself into anything else? Hell, you've got a design diploma, and Liz can sing, and Nancy's studying this philology bit—you've got the *chance* to be something other than a lady of leisure."

"Strikes me you're trying to live down the stigma of being a gentleman yourself," Glenn grunted. "That's one problem I'm never going to have to cope with."

"I wouldn't mind being a lady of leisure," Nancy shrugged.

"I'll bet you wouldn't like being one without any choice, and having no funds to support you," Gideon countered. "No, Bruno is damned right."

"So it's an unjust world," Glenn said. "That's news? All you can hope to do about it is spread a little more love than there was before you came on the scene. What should we do to fix Miss Beeding—buy her a crate of beer, for charity?"

"Christ, there's no need to make us all feel morbid," Cress said, reaching past Nancy to switch the radio on. It was playing music again by now. She jumped to her feet and kicked her sandals aside.

"I think I'll go for a swim," she announced. "It'd be a shame to come to the seaside and not get a bathe in."

"The water may not be very clean around here," Bruno warned. "You heard what the cat at the research station said about pollution."

"Pollution schmollution. It probably isn't any worse than London air."

"No, you've got a point there."

"So are you coming?"

"You go scout the water and tell me if it's warm and clean. Then maybe I'll join you."

Cress made a face at him and began to unbutton her shirt. "Nobody else? Gid?"

"I'm happy here," Gideon said, leaning sideways to rest his cheek against Nancy's shoulder.

"Glenn?"

The American shook his head. "Guess I'll just take a stroll around the beach and pick up some more wood for the fire."

"I'll come," Liz offered, tugging down the long front zipper of her dress and slipping out of it. Underneath, she wore matched bra and panties in vivid tangerine-yellow; the light of the fire made her skin almost the same shade.

She added to Cress, "Want to take the torch?"

"I don't think so—we'd have to put it down somewhere and it might be difficult to find again. It's still light enough to see pretty well over there." She unhooked her bra and placed it on her neatly folded slacks. "I'm going to take everything off, aren't you? There isn't anyone to see, and I don't want to spoil these undies. They're much too nice."

"It's squelchy," Liz said as she picked her way over the beach a yard behind Cress. "I hate the feel of mud between my toes."

"It's all right here," Cress reported. "Quite firm. And not too much weed, either." She splashed her first few paces into the water. "It's warm, too—thought it would be. Lovely!"

"Watch out for oil, though," Liz warned. "Lots of ships go past here."

"We could always clean up with a drop of petrol from the van," Cress said. "I do hope we manage to lay on this freakout of Glenn's, don't you? It'd be terrific out here! Can't you just imagine light projectors on all those chalk surfaces, and huge great amplifiers hung on the top of the cliff? Fab!"

By now they had gotten far enough out to swim. Cress, the better swimmer of the two, plunged forward and raced out to sea with an easy professional crawl. Liz hung back a little, paddling around where it was still shallow enough for her to stand. The night was quiet, and with the setting of the sun the twilight glow had faded except where the vast lights of London were diffused to the westward. Faintly from the neighborhood of the fire there came the sound of music.

Satisfied that the water was fairly clean, Liz turned on her back and floated for a while, staring up at the stars.

Suddenly, however, she heard a splashing noise not far away, and rolled over, thinking Cress must be coming back. But she could still see the other girl, a long way out, and the splashing had come from closer by. She strained her eyes, puzzled, to see if she could spot the source, and finally detected a movement at the edge of the water. Something on all fours was awkwardly emerging.

"A dog?" she said half-aloud. It was about the right size—not much larger than the Ridgeback they had seen earlier. But it seemed to be moving awkwardly, perhaps from injury, and hesitated every few seconds as though summoning up energy for its next heave toward the beach.

Injured or not, however, a dog would probably have its master somewhere nearby, and they were swimming nude. She called low and urgently over the water: "Cress! Cress, come here!"

Obediently the other girl put her head down and came briskly swimming inshore.

"Look!" Liz said, pointing. "There's a dog or something coming out of the sea there. Somebody may be with it."

"So what?" Cress said cheerfully, shaking back her wet hair. "They don't have to look at us if they don't want to."

"Well, I think I'm going back anyway. I've had enough. It is nice and warm but I got a mouthful and it doesn't taste very good."

Cress sighed. "Okay, just as you like. Actually I only wanted to cool down a bit, myself."

Together they emerged from the sea and hurried back to where they had left their clothes, glancing occasionally at the half-seen dark creature struggling in the shallows.

"If it is a dog, it must be hurt," Cress said suddenly.

"That's exactly what I thought," Liz agreed. "I suppose we'd better go over and see when we've got dressed."

"I don't want to put my clothes on while I'm still wet," Cress objected. "I was going to run around the beach and dry off first."

"I put a whole stack of paper napkins in the lunch-basket," Liz said. "They'll do for towels. Come on."

Beside the fire they found only Gideon and Nancy sitting together companionably, his arm around her shoulders, listening to a Dylan number on the radio. "Enjoy it?" Gideon demanded as they began to share out the paper napkins and rub themselves dry.

"Sort of," Liz answered. "But there's an injured dog or something coming out of the water. We're going back to see to it."

"Where are the others?" Cress demanded.

"Gone to look for more wood, they said. Maybe they'll see this dog, or whatever."

"Now that's a great phrase!" Nancy said suddenly; she was concentrating on the radio. "It's this ritual bit Dylan gets that I like so much. There's this pattern of associations. . . ."

They wandered off into an argument about the semantic overtones of words from various root languages, which the others couldn't follow. It was Gideon's interest in song-writing that had originally brought him together with Nancy, who was studying philology, and they seemed to spend half their time discussing technicalities connected with perfectly ordinary words, which Gideon claimed he needed to know about in order to give the songs he composed for the group their maximum impact.

Cress and Liz were dry quickly, except for Cress's hair, which was thicker and longer than Liz's, and began to put their clothes back on. Both were in their undies and were reaching for the rest of their garments when there was a sudden frantic call from Glenn, way off in the darkness.

"Hey! There's someone here! He's hurt!"

Holding her dress ready to step into, Liz froze. She stared at Cress.

"Could it have been a *man* we saw?"

"Going on hands and knees—Christ, maybe it was!" Cress dropped her slacks back on the rock and darted off. Liz threw her dress down also and followed, while Gideon and Nancy were scrambling to their feet.

Out of the dark Bruno came hurrying, his feet splashing in the shallow water. "Glenn, is he badly hurt?" he demanded. "Can he talk?"

"Hasn't said anything yet," Glenn panted, bending over the sprawled form in the sea. "Here, help me get him on his feet!"

Bruno stared down. There was a curious *softness* about the outline of the injured man, as though he had been deformed under pressure, but there was no doubt that he was alive and badly hurt. He hastened to join Glenn in raising the man to his feet, finding the touch of his arm clammy and a little slimy.

His deformed appearance was apparently due to the fact that he was wearing some kind of leathery, close-fitting garment that had filled with water during his immersion. He was medium-tall and of average build—it was too dark to make out more detail—but the water made him improbably heavy, and he seemed too dazed to cooperate, so it was only with the greatest difficulty that they managed to lift him upright. They achieved it finally, and he stood swaying a little, one arm over Glenn's shoulders and one over Bruno's.

"Have you got him?" Liz called as they stood panting with the effort, ready to lead the injured man forward to their fire. She and Cress came dashing up, their pale bodies glimmering in the darkness.

"Yes, but he hasn't made a sound," Glenn said.

"Maybe he's fallen overboard from a ship, and he's in shock," Cress said. "Let's get him over to the fire and dry him out a bit. Careful, though—he may have bones broken, or anything."

"Come on, feller," Bruno said, and urged the man forward. Awkwardly, as though he had exhausted every muscle, he took first one stumbling step, then another, draping on their shoulders as on a pair of crutches.

"Jesus God!" Bruno said without warning, and freed himself, leaping back with a look of horror.

Glenn snapped, "Bruno, what in hell are you playing at? Come back!"

"But that guy's not breathing!" Bruno said. "Hell, can't you feel with the arm you've got around him? He's *not breathing*!"

"But drowned people can't move at all," Liz said stupidly. "Can they?"

Glenn abruptly did the same as Bruno, white-faced and shaking. "You're damn right!" he whispered. "I can't feel him breathe, either!"

In the same instant they heard the sound of Gideon's and Nancy's footsteps, hurrying to join them. Gideon had brought the flashlight with him. He snapped it on, and it fell full on the face of the man from the sea as he swayed uncertainly, drunk-fashion, on his sodden legs.

Or, rather, on his half-face. Puffy with incipient decomposition, his hideous pallid flesh looked more like sponge; one blank blue eye stretched wide as a fish's regarded them, but the other was closed, while below it the cheek was eaten away to reveal the whiteness of bone and teeth.

V

THEIR COLLECTIVE NERVE lasted about three seconds. Then one of the girls screamed—or it could have been all of them hitting exactly the same shrill note—and they stumbled away from the impossible stranger. He made to come after them but lost his footing, trying to take a colossally long stride and overbalancing. He slumped forward, still in the beam of the torch, and what seemed to be endless gallons of water poured from his mouth and nose.

Without stopping to reclaim their belongings, they fled, panicking, toward the path that led up from the beach to the field above. Even Gideon turned and ran with them, but he halted suddenly and called out.

"Stop! Stop! Come back!"

None of the others listened, but went on scrambling up the path.

In the level field at the top, with the van's parking lights faintly visible beyond the gate they had climbed to get here, everything suddenly seemed more normal. The Kentish countryside was quiet around them: familiar, unthreatening. Feeling rather foolish, they stopped and stared at one another, and Cress said something about treading on a thistle with her bare feet.

"For Chrissake, you lot!" Gideon called, waving the torch as he finally made his way up the path to rejoin them. "Wait for it, wait for it!"

Back on the beach, for a few moments the stranger lay still, gasping out the last of the water from his mouth and nose. After a short while his limbs began to stir again. With painful slowness he forced himself to his feet; he raised one foot, then the other, this time planting them a controllable distance apart. Almost mechanically, uttering terrible wheezing noises, he crossed the beach and began to plod through the shallow water around the headland.

"Hell's *name*!" Gideon panted as he came up to the others. "What made you take to your heels like that?"

Very pale, Cress said, "But you—you *saw* him, didn't you?"

"All right, the poor bastard's hurt! He's horribly and disgustingly hurt! But he's *alive*, isn't he? He's got to be taken to a hospital, fast! Christ, Bruno, why did you have to start that crazy panic about him not breathing?"

"I tell you I felt him—felt his body!" Bruno snapped. "So did Glenn!"

"What do you think he is, then—a zombie, maybe? Man, I don't even believe in zombies back home, let alone here in England! He moved, didn't he? He even walked a few steps?"

The others nodded.

"Well, then! Like Liz said, drowned men can't move— ergo he isn't drowned. We got to get right back down there and help him over to the van. Come on!"

Gideon whirled and made for the path again. The other two men exchanged glances.

"He's right," Bruno said after a pause. "Here, you girls grab your clothes and pack up the rest of the gear, hm? We'll see to this character. Let's go, Glenn."

But when they caught up with Gideon, who was shining the flashlight around with a puzzled expression, there was no sign of the stranger except some scuffed marks that might have been the trail of dragging feet.

"You know something?" Gideon said as the other two joined him. "I wonder if I got stoned without remembering. Did I?"

"Where's he gone?" Glenn demanded.

"Baby, you're asking *me*?" Gideon countered. "You see if you can spot him!"

They spread out, without another word, and searched the entire beach. When they regrouped at the spot where they had left the stranger, they all shook their heads.

"Nothing," Glenn said.

"Have you got him yet?" came a tremulous call from Cress, in the distance. "We're all packed up and ready to go, here!"

Gideon led the way toward the fire, switching off the flashlight as they came into its glow. He said curtly, "No sign of him. Vanished. Must have thought we weren't going to help him, and gone looking for someone else."

They all looked embarrassedly at one another.

"We'll have to report this," Bruno said suddenly. "Maybe they can find him before—well, before he drops in his tracks. He looked just about all in."

"You mean like to the fuzz?" Glenn snapped. "I don't care to have too much to do with them."

"Stuff that!" Bruno said. "This could mean a man's life, couldn't it? What's become of that love you want to spread around, baby?"

"I guess you're right," Glenn shrugged.

"Let's move, then!" Gideon exclaimed, and picked up the empty picnic basket.

VI

FIVE MINUTES AFTER his favorite pub closed for the night at ten-thirty, Joseph Leigh-Warden walked into the Brindown police station as he usually did on his way home. He was not an attractive man any longer, though in his youth he had been quite handsome. Too much beer—which made his breath stink tonight, as every night—and congenital laziness had made him fat and given him a red nose. But he was good at his job, after his own fashion.

The young constable on duty at the inquiry desk looked up at his visitor, incongruously dressed in an open-necked shirt with a silk foulard, a tweed jacket with leather patches on the elbows, and gray flannel trousers which his increasing paunch compelled him to wear so low that their bottoms were frayed on the heels of his shoes, and said without noticeable enthusiasm, "Good evening, Mr. Warden."

"The name is Leigh-Warden, if you don't mind! Got anything for me this evening?"

"I don't think so," the young constable said, adding with calculated lateness: "*Sir!* It's been a quiet evening, apart from a couple of drunks who started a fight outside the Red Bull. Sergeant Branksome is dealing with them now."

Leigh-Warden scowled and sat down on the visitors' bench opposite the desk. "Well, I'll hang on to have a word with him, anyhow," he muttered. "By the way, tell me *your* name again, will you?"

"I'm Constable Sellers, sir," the policeman said tiredly. He was getting bored with Leigh-Warden's constant gibes. It seemed to be the same routine every night he was on duty.

"Yes, of course," Leigh-Warden grunted. "Well! Want a cigarette?"

"No, thank you. I still don't smoke. And if you don't mind, I have a report to type up." Defiantly, Sellers made for the typewriter on its metal table behind the inquiry desk.

"You're not going to get ahead in your job unless you cooperate with the press, young feller-me-lad!" Leigh-Warden said.

"I haven't any cooperation to offer tonight, sir," Sellers answered, noisily rattling paper and carbons into the machine. "Like I said, it's been a quiet evening. . . . Ah, here comes Sergeant Branksome now!" he added with obvious relief.

"Oh, you're here, are you?" the sergeant said as he emerged from the charge-room door across the narrow hallway of the station. "Evening! Nothing much for you tonight, though—Sellers probably told you, didn't he?"

"Drunks having a bash at each other, he said," Leigh-Warden shrugged. "Who were they?"

"A couple of the laborers who were working on the new fish-pond or whatever it is they put in at the marine research station. Determined to drink their back pay before going to look for another job, I suppose." The sergeant pushed his fingers wearily through his short brown hair. He looked tired, and older than his age of thirty.

"Irish again?" Leigh-Warden suggested.

"I don't know what you mean about *again*," the sergeant snapped.

"It's the Irish that make the trouble around here, and the teenage yobs who come down from London. Isn't that the truth?" Leigh-Warden scowled.

"You ought to be bloody grateful to them," Branksome retorted. "It's thanks to them you get your snippets in the London papers, isn't it? Can't imagine the Fleet Street boys paying you for flower-show prize lists, or Women's Institute meeting reports!"

"There's no need to be offensive," Leigh-Warden said stiffly.

"Sorry, but I'm tired," the sergeant muttered. "It's been a long, hard day. . . . *Now* what?"

They all turned as, in the doorway, a young man appeared, wearing an open striped windbreaker over a shirt which was stained with mud and wet. He paused uncertainly on the threshold; then, spotting Branksome's chevrons, addressed him.

"Sergeant, something very odd has happened that you probably ought to know about!"

Branksome pulled himself together with obvious effort. He said, "Well, we're always obliged when members of the public report suspicious events—Sellers! What are you staring at like a dead fish?"

The constable, whose gaze had fixed on the new arrival in fascination, gulped and looked apologetic.

"Sorry, sarge! But I think I know who this—this gentleman is. Aren't you Bruno? From Bruno and the Hermetic Tradition? I've seen you on the telly!"

Bruno gave an embarrassed grin and nodded. "Well, yes, but that's nothing to do with what I called in about. Look, there seems to be a sick man—badly hurt, not just sick—wandering around on the beach near here, and we tried to get hold of him and take him to a hospital and—well, we didn't make it. He—uh—he ran off. But he's so badly hurt somebody ought to find him."

Sergeant Branksome tensed. He said, "Can you describe this man?"

"Well—ah . . ." Bruno swallowed hard. "About medium height, I suppose, wearing some kind of—well, what looked like a motorcycling outfit, I guess. Like with zippers and boots. I didn't see very clearly. It was dark on the beach. But you couldn't mistake him." He shuddered as he raised his clawed hand to indicate his cheek. "All his face is—well—kind of eaten away around here, from the cheekbone to the bottom of the jaw!"

There was silence for several seconds. During it, Leigh-Warden walked to the door and peered out. He stayed there, staring, while Branksome recovered.

"Motorcycling outfit," he repeated. "Could it have been a flying-suit?"

"I guess it could," Bruno agreed. "Why, is someone missing?"

"There was a plane that came down—"

"Sarge, that was days ago!" Sellers objected. "They gave the pilot up for dead, didn't they?"

"I suppose he could have been drifting, exhausted, and got carried ashore," Branksome said. "Where exactly was this?"

"I don't know the name of the place. But it was on a bit of beach with a chalk cliff overhanging it," Bruno said. "Oh—and an old lady called Miss Beeding lives nearby. She spoke to us."

"That'll be about halfway between here and Geddesley," Sellers offered. "We know the old bag, don't we, sarge?"

"Too well," Branksome grunted. "She's spent every Saturday night here for months! Then we just quietly lose her on Sunday morning. She's no special trouble—just gets a bit merry when she's got a drop inside her. No point in fining her because she can't pay, and as for putting her inside—!"

Leigh-Warden turned back from the door with a triumphant expression. He said, "Constable Sellers, how did you know about this—ah—visitor?"

"Saw him with his group, on 'Top of the Pops,'" Sellers said. "I don't imagine you watch that very much, sir!"

"Oh, but I do," Leigh-Warden contradicted. "Wasn't it a song about a diver and a dolphin that they recorded?"

Bruno glanced at him. "That's right," he admitted. "*Seadeath*."

"*Seadeath!*" Leigh-Warden's eyes gleamed. "And it's a sea death of a kind you've called in about, hm?"

"I don't get you," Bruno said, looking puzzled.

"With your permission, sergeant, I'd like to ask what this group was doing on the beach where they found this—this alleged person!"

"Oh, go ahead," Branksome sighed tiredly.

"We were—ah—having a picnic," Bruno said. "Three of us from the group, and our girl-friends. Not doing any harm to anyone!"

"Getting stoned, were you?" Leigh-Warden rapped. "Having delusions?"

"Shit!" Bruno burst out. "I tell you we *saw* this man—all of us did! Think we were on acid, or something?"

"Ah, 'acid,'" Leigh-Warden echoed. "You mean LSD, don't you? Well, maybe it was hashish or marijuana—I know what pop groups are like!"

"Listen, baby!" Bruno stepped up to him, clenching his fists. "While you're throwing insults around there's a man out there who needs help—for all I know he's dying!"

Leigh-Warden curled his lip. "Is that so? Suffering a sea death, hm?" He turned to Branksome. "Sergeant, I think this is a bad publicity stunt, don't you? Either that, or they were taking some kind of drug that causes hallucinations. Because a man with his face eaten away from cheekbone to jawbone wouldn't be alive, after drifting in the sea ever since—when was it that plane crashed? Three days ago, four? He'd be dead from loss of blood, wouldn't he?"

Branksome hesitated. He said at length, "I'm afraid I couldn't say. I don't know enough about medicine to be sure."

"Take my word for it," Leigh-Warden declared.

"Not yet," Branksome said after further thought. "I think we ought at least to check on this. Rodge, go out with them to the place where they saw him and look around. If you think it's worth following up, phone in, okay?"

"Right, sarge," Sellers said with alacrity, seizing his helmet from the wall-peg where it was hanging.

"But this cat may be dying!" Bruno said again.

"Sir, I'm afraid I'm not prepared to turn out the entire Kent county constabulary on a midnight search!" Branksome said in an ill-tempered voice.

"But—!" Bruno checked, and made to turn away dejectedly. "Okay okay! We'll see if we can track him down."

"You have transport?" Branksome said suddenly.

"They do indeed," Leigh-Warden told him, chuckling. "It's across the street. A positive bloody nightmare on wheels, believe me!"

"I suppose you run a gold-plated Rolls?" Bruno snapped.

For an instant, he thought the reporter was going to hit him, but he settled for a sneer and marched out. Constable Sellers headed after him, and Bruno, looking miserable, followed on.

VII

"THIS MAKES A change from just sitting in the station all night, anyhow," Constable Sellers said. Glenn had crammed himself into the back of the van with the others, and the policeman had taken his place next to Cress on the front seat. He didn't seem to mind sitting beside a pretty girl in mod clothes, either.

Watching the road ahead in the glare of the iodine-quartz spotlights he had had fitted for their frequent trips overnight from gig to gig, Bruno muttered, "I got a pretty cold reception, though, didn't I?"

"That wasn't us, sir," Sellers said apologetically.

"What's with this 'sir' bit?" Glenn demanded from the back.

"Regulation—kind of," Sellers said.

"Well, forget it for my sake, hm? I'm Glenn—Glenn Salmon. Who are you?"

"Well—ah—my name's Roger, actually. People call me Rodge."

"So okay then. Who was it who gave Bruno this bad reception, Rodge?"

"He's a reporter of sorts. Pompous stuffy bastard. He's good at his job, they say, but he's bloody unlikable. And he can't be that good or he'd be on a London paper instead of working as a local stringer. Mostly he sells juicy write-ups of scandal cases—you know: 'Holiday Wife-Trading Led to Divorce'?" He sighed. "Wish he hadn't been there! The sarge is quite a decent guy, really. But he overworks. He's a sad case—wife walked out on him because she couldn't stand the hours he came home. So he wears himself out to keep his mind off it, I suppose."

"And what *was* the cold reception?" Gideon demanded.

"Bastard tried to make out we were all stoned!" Bruno said.

Sellers coughed. "I—ah—I suppose you aren't risking . . . ?" He hesitated. "Look, I'm sort of a fan of yours, and I have a couple of records you've made, so . . ."

"Human, yet!" Glenn muttered.

"If what you're getting at"—Bruno slid the van around a fast curve, the tires at the back complaining and the passengers having to grab for support—"is asking whether we do have drugs on board, the answer is: shit, *no*! I wouldn't carry hash or pot on this van even if I liked it, which I don't. It'd shoot our roster of gigs to hell if we were held up on some goddamned possession charge! We couldn't afford it. It's tough scuffling making the four dates a week we need to live on, what with the distances we have to travel. It'll be okay when our records start to sell better, but right now it's not easy."

Sellers gave a sigh of relief. "That's good to know. Because the sarge did seem to take it seriously when that bugger Leigh-Warden suggested you'd had some kind of a delusion. Though," he added hastily, "I'm sure he wouldn't have acted that way if he weren't so dead beat."

He shifted on the seat with a muttered query to Cress about being comfortable; when she said she was fine, he went on, "This whole thing is rather queer, though! See, earlier in the week there was this plane crash near here— you read about it?"

"Of course!" Gideon said. "Saw on telly all these rescue boats, and dredgers and things! Was that near here?"

"About eight miles west, towards Whitstable—at least that's what they think." Sellers shrugged. "It was a big search and we were kept pretty busy liaising because we're halfway between the two extreme limits of the area where the plane must have hit. But I don't see how it could have been the pilot you found! He *must* be dead by now—poor devil."

"He looked dead," Bruno muttered.

"What?"

"I said he looked dead!" Bruno repeated. "But I could hardly come right out in the police station there and say: 'This guy we fished out of the water wasn't breathing!' I mean, *could* I?"

There was a depressed silence until the gate beside the copse, which was their landmark to locate the beach again, loomed up in the brilliant glare of the lights. Bruno braked hard.

"Right!" he said, throwing open the driver's door. "Let's go see what we can find!"

And the answer was—nothing.

Except what they expected. Their fire was still burning merrily and Gideon threw some more of the driest wood on it to give extra light. From it, they retraced the direction in which Glenn had found the man from the sea, and showed Sellers the scuffed footmarks leading inshore, then out again: three sets, then one. But the tide was on the turn now, and by morning it was clear that no trace would be left.

"I hate to tell you this," Sellers said at length, when they grouped around the fire after their search. "But you know what I'm going to have to say to the sergeant, don't you?"

"That it was a load of nonsense," Liz suggested.

"Well, I'll make it as mild as I can, of course! But—there isn't much to go on, is there?"

"I suppose not," Bruno admitted. "But if the poor

49

so-and-so turns up dead on some other bit of beach in the morning, I'm not going to feel very pleased with myself. And I doubt if you are, either!"

"Look, sir—I mean, *Bruno*. Put yourself in my place. Somebody walks out of the night and—"

"See any roaches around here?" Gideon demanded fiercely, stepping up to him. "See any hypodermics? See any sugar lumps, blotting paper, problematical artifacts?"

"Proble— What?" Sellers blinked at him.

"Problematical artifacts! That's what the fuzz in the States call things like—oh—a matchbook rolled up to make a holder for a joint!" Gideon was furious; his friends could tell by his tone of voice, but he was perfectly controlled outwardly. "Get this, baby! We were not drunk, we were not blocked, we were not anything except kind of happy because we were having a real swinging picnic on a beach on a fine summer evening! And some very sick cat came up out of the water and right this instant he's probably weeping his life away around that headland there!"

"Couldn't it have been—well—someone out for a late swim who . . . ?" Sellers hesitated and swallowed loudly. "No, I suppose not. Well, all I can say is, I'm very sorry. But I must tell the sarge exactly what I've seen, and that's—that's a fire and some footmarks!"

"Gid, calm down," Bruno said in a weary voice. "Rodge is perfectly right. Anyway, he—"

He checked. From the cliff-top above a shadowy figure was leaning over, silhouetted against the stars.

A thick voice said, "Got him, have you?" A chuckle followed.

"That's the reporter I saw in the police station," Bruno muttered to his companions. More loudly, he called: "No, we didn't find him! Are you satisfied?"

"I'm always satisfied to find that I was right," Leigh-

Warden answered, and moved away. When they climbed despondently back from the beach, they saw the lights of another car fading into the distance.

They dropped off Sellers at the police station and drove straight off toward the London road. They had left the town completely before anyone spoke; then Nancy said suddenly, "He looked so *horrible*! I'm going to have nightmares about him, I'm sure I am!"

"No, you're not, baby," Gideon said, putting his arm reassuringly around her shoulders.

"Tell you what I'm going to dream about," Glenn said sourly. "Your goddamned English complacency!"

"Stuff it!" Bruno said. "The busy we gave the lift to was decent enough, wasn't he? It's only this bloody official inertia that makes the trouble. . . . But I've had enough arguments for one night. Cress, put the radio on and let's cheer ourselves up a bit, hm?"

To the blasting, joyous noise of the Beatles, the van plunged down the dark road toward London.

"Well?" Branksome demanded, as Sellers reentered the station.

Hanging up his helmet, the young constable frowned. "I don't know what to say, sarge," he admitted. "We didn't find anything, and in the dark I doubt honestly if anyone could have searched more thoroughly than we did. But—"

"But what? Were they having delusions, or lying, or what?"

"Sarge, I don't think they were." Sellers drew a deep breath. "There were these three birds with them in the van, and I kept an eye on them, you see. If they'd been trying to put something over on us, they'd have given it away at some point, wouldn't they? But they seemed to be genuinely upset!"

"So what happened to this man they claimed to have found?"

"From what they told me about his behavior, he was quite crazy enough to have gone back in the sea of his own accord," Sellers said.

"I see." Branksome hesitated. "Well, in that case we'd better follow it up, I suppose. They have withdrawn the search vessels, though, haven't they?"

"Yes, they called them off last night when they gave up hope of finding the pilot."

"Well, even so there'll be the regular coast-guard patrols, and Customs ought to hear about it just in case, and all the other local stations and lifeboat stations. And county headquarters, and even the marine research station ought to be told, I suppose."

"I'll see to that, sarge," Sellers offered. "You look all in!"

Branksome nodded. "That's very kind of you. I am dead beat. So I'll see you in the morning, then. Good night."

The phone rang. Inkosi jumped up and started to bark. Tom Reedwall snapped at him to be quiet and spat out the toothpaste from his mouth. Behind him, Netta— already in bed in a filmy black nightdress—glanced up from her book.

"What on earth could that be?" she demanded.

"I'll go and find out," Tom muttered, rinsing his mouth and reaching for a towel to wipe his lips.

Shortly he came back from the phone, shrugging.

"It's about the pilot of the crashed plane," he said. "Seems someone reported seeing him trying to get up the beach, but lost him again."

"It's impossible!" Netta declared. "If he'd lived this long, he'd have been found by the search parties already! He must have drowned, or been cast ashore long before now."

"I'm just telling you what they said," Tom grunted, peeling off his shirt and reaching for his pajamas. "They wanted us to keep an eye out, of course. But I'm shot if I'm going to stand out on the beach all night because of some unconfirmed rumor."

He added with a deliberate leer, "Me, I don't even believe in mermaids. Why should I? I've got what I want."

"You're a darling," Netta said with a chuckle, and put her book aside.

In the tumbledown, half-burned farmhouse abandoned by its original owner where she had taken up residence, Miss Felicia Beeding sat rocking back and forth on a chair with one arm missing. Around her the squalor was appalling: old newspapers were draped over the furniture and spread across the floor, the windows were partly stopped by bits of cardboard and old rags, and there was no light except what came from a flickering oil lamp. The empty beer bottle the visitors had given her was tipped over alongside her chair. On an empty stomach—for she had eaten nothing today except for a crust at breakfast-time—it had been enough to make her drowsy.

There was a tapping at the door. She roused from her stupor.

"Kitty-kitty!" she said automatically, then stopped herself and frowned. Elegance, the tomcat who had been her companion for seven lonely years, had been run over by a car months ago and she had carried his carcass weeping to a grave in the chalky earth behind the house.

"So it can't be Elegance wanting to come in," she said aloud as she forced her old bones out of the chair. "But maybe it's another cat wanting to keep a poor old woman company! Wouldn't that be nice, now? To have a stranger come out of the night and purr through the door!"

Beaming, she steadied herself with a quick snatch at the wall.

"Or perhaps it's those nice young people come back to say thank you for being allowed to picnic here," she reasoned. "Goodness, it's amazing to find such good manners nowadays! It would be dreadfully ungracious of me not to answer the door, wouldn't it, Elegance—? Oh, no. Of course. You're not here, are you?"

There was a cracked mirror on the wall, hanging from a slanted nail. It had fallen down twice, but it still showed her fly-specked reflection. Before it she paused and automatically touched her hair, not seeing the image of her present self but an earlier, younger Miss Beeding who had captivated the gallant Captain Horder and would have married him if he hadn't been killed in action. She went past the mirror, having spent less than a heartbeat looking into it, and opened the door, raising the oil lamp to see who the caller might be.

Ten seconds later, she screamed, and the lamp went crashing to the floor.

VIII

THE PHONE ROUSED Bruno from an uneasy slumber in which he had dreamed of walking on water following footprints he dared not tread on himself because they would give way and let him drown.

Struggling back to awareness, he vaguely heard Cress say, "I'll get it!" And, after another few moments, he realized she was holding the phone toward him, saying, "For you—it's Monty."

Trying to control a yawn, Bruno put the receiver to his ear. "Coffee ready?" he demanded of Cress.

"Percolating now," she said, and went into the adjacent kitchen to check it.

"Yeah, Monty?" Bruno said. "What's with you at this unearthly hour of the morning?"

"Nearly ten, baby—some of us have been at it for a while already. But what's with this bit in the paper, that's what I want to know!"

"Hell, Monty, your call woke me up. *What* bit in the paper?"

"Here, listen." Rustling noises. " 'Bruno Twentyman, of the Hermetic Tradition pop group, tonight claimed that members of his band had located the missing test pilot who crashed off the Kent coast last Monday. A search by police at the scene of the alleged discovery, however, revealed nothing, and a police spokesman later said, quote, the report was either a hoax or a hallucination. The search for the missing man was called off at dark yesterday, by which time experts estimated that he must defin-itely be dead.' Look, baby, what were you trying to do—nose *Seadeath* back to the charts, or something?"

"That son of a bitch," Bruno said between his teeth, pushing himself to an upright position. "God damn, Mon-ty, give me credit for more sense than that, won't you? We never said anything about finding the missing pilot! What happened was simply that an injured man came up the beach where we were picnicking, and we decided to try and get him to hospital, but he disappeared, and we thought we ought to report it."

"So who put this decorated version about, baby?"

"A bloated pig of a local stringer who was in the fuzzbox when I called there. Name of Leigh-Warden. Look, have we friends on the staff of the paper that printed it?"

"I have friends everywhere," Monty grunted. "Of a sort."

"See if you can get them to climb down. On principle. If even you jumped to that conclusion—"

"What do you mean, *I* jumped to it? Think I've had time to check the news-in-brief columns today? It was Brian Harvey from Luxor who called me first. You know how stuffy they are over there."

Bruno's heart sank. Luxor was not a large recording company, but it was the first that had offered the group a decent commercial contract, and Monty had recently been negotiating a first LP for them.

"What he didn't like, of course, was the hallucination bit," Monty pursued. "Said it could be read to mean you were all stoned."

"Think it wasn't meant to?" Bruno muttered. "But—like—could you make a libel writ stick on it?"

"Nope. At least I doubt it very much. Just don't do it again, is all."

"And leave some poor bugger to die on his own? I'm telling you, Monty, that was a badly injured man we saw."

"What were you doing on a Kent beach, anyway? Was it the one Glenn wanted to hold a freakout on?"

"Right. We had some trouble finding it, but it would suit fine."

"Well, drop the idea for the moment, will you? Or someone might complain about your hoaxing the police to get publicity for the project, and believe me, baby, the busies are trouble enough without them starting to imagine they're being used for PR purposes!"

"Shit, Monty, go put your head under a cold tap, hm? You sound like you're developing a persecution complex!" Bruno slammed down the phone.

Cress, appearing from the kitchen with coffee mugs in both hands, said, "What was all that about?"

Bruno summarized it for her.

"It's a sick bloody world, isn't it?" he concluded. But she gave him a long grave stare.

"If we hadn't panicked . . ." she said finally.

"I know. I'm ashamed of myself. Only Gid kept his head. I don't know what happened to me. Except that he really looked so revolting he was more like something from a bad trip than a—than a casualty. I don't know if Nancy had nightmares, but I did."

"So did I," Cress muttered, and sipped her coffee.

The phone rang again. Bruno seized it. "Yes?"

Cress asked a question with her eyes; covering the mouthpiece briefly, he said, "Dick Marvell from the Mellow Cellar. We're working there tonight, remember?" More loudly, he went on, "Morning, Dick. Did you manage to set—?"

"Hold it, baby," said the distant voice. "Seen the papers today?"

"Christ. No, I haven't! But Monty just called and read it over to me. So?"

"Hell, Bruno, you know what a bloody job we have keeping the fuzz off our necks here at the Cellar—making people sign declarations they aren't bringing pot into the premises, and like that. They've turned us over twice already, you know, without finding anything. You've just about certified that we'll have 'em back tonight."

"*I* did?" Furious, Bruno swung his feet out of bed. "Now you listen to me, will you?"

Sympathetically, Cress rescued his coffee before he knocked it to the floor and went to prepare breakfast.

It was like that most of the morning.

"This was the place they brought me to," Roger Sellers said over his shoulder. "Parked their van there—see the tire marks on the verge?"

He swung his scooter around and halted it alongside the gate through which Bruno had taken him last night. Behind him on the pillion, Doreen Swale stared with wide-eyed fascination at the tracks he had pointed out.

Privately, he thought she was rather silly, but she was very young—not yet eighteen—and certainly she was extremely pretty. He could think of much worse ways of spending a couple of off-duty hours than taking her out to show her where one of her favorite pop groups had had a beach picnic.

"I wish I'd *known!*" she said for the umpteenth time.

Sellers looked rather sour, but kept his face turned away.

"Can we go down and look at the beach?" Doreen demanded.

"There won't be much to see—the tide will have been up since they were there."

"I'd like to look anyway," she countered obstinately,

and jumped off the pillion seat with her miniskirt practically up to her waist. She was wearing a black straw sombrero, which had given endless trouble during the ride, and a miniature transistor radio hung from her left wrist like a bangle. She turned it on while waiting for him to prop the scooter up, and an announcer said clearly, "Now the latest news from Radio Jolly Roger!"

Grimacing, she switched it off again. "Nothing so jolly about you, is there?" she said after a pause.

"Please, I've heard it before," Sellers said with a wince. "But—well, no, I'm not very cheerful, am I? I can't help wondering about what Bruno said. I mean, for all I know we're quite likely to find a dead body on the beach here!"

"You didn't find anything last night, though, did you?" Doreen shrugged, inspecting the padlock on the gate. When she saw it was tightly fastened, she climbed over agilely. Sellers followed, took her hand, and led her across the field.

The beach, as he'd expected, had been washed clean by the night's tide. He stood silently alongside her, waiting for her to finish extracting what reflected glamour she could from the place where some of her idols had briefly stopped for their picnic, and was relieved when she turned away.

"What's that place over there?" she said suddenly, raising her arm.

"Oh, the old Warrinder farmhouse," Sellers answered. "It got burned out eight or ten years ago. There's a funny old lady who sort of camps out in it. Miss Beeding."

"Goodness, imagine living in a ruin like that!" Doreen started to walk toward it, and he perforce followed, not much relishing having to meet and talk to the old nuisance if she proved to be at home. "Why, it's practically— Rodge!"

He had darted past her, halting twenty yards ahead, staring at the shell of the old house, and sniffing the air.

"Smoke!" he exclaimed. "Lord, can she have set the place on fire again?"

The single remaining door was askew on its hinges. Cautiously he peered through. Yes, there was definitely a smell of recent burning.

"You keep back," he told Doreen. "I've often thought the old bag might set her home alight with one of her oil lamps. . . . My God, what a pigsty!"

He entered warily, bracing himself for the shock of finding Miss Beeding burned to death. There was a huge blackened patch spreading from the middle of this, the former farm kitchen, which because of its tiled floor had survived the original fire better than the rest of the house. Partly burned newspapers were draped over the sticks of furniture, clothing them in shrouds of fragile black ash. In the middle of the room there was a broken oil lamp. He prodded it gingerly with his toe, seeing that the chimney was smashed.

But the fire had not been hot enough to ignite anything except the newspapers. By a minor miracle, it had failed to heat up the two-gallon oil drum that he found propped in one corner on a stack of bricks. That would have exploded like a bomb if the flames had reached it.

He went out of the room on the far side, finding himself in a passage partly roofed with the weather-rotted floorboards of what had been an upstairs room. Some pieces of polyethylene and various rags had been crudely nailed over this area. At the end of the passage he found a filthy, stinking privy, whose door he hastily shut after making certain Miss Beeding wasn't trapped in there.

Returning with a puzzled expression, he called to Doreen.

"No sign of her! Maybe she ran off when the fire started. I suppose I ought to ask at the other houses nearby."

"But surely if she'd turned up somewhere shouting fire, they'd have sent for the fire brigade?" Doreen objected.

He revised his opinion about her silliness a little. "That's a very good point," he admitted. "Should have thought of it myself. And there isn't any sign of fire engines coming this way. They'd have had to open the gate we climbed over, for a start."

He bit his lip. "Anyway, I'd probably have been notified," he concluded.

There was a long silence, during which Doreen surveyed the mess and shuddered. He was just old enough to remember the aftermath of the war, when there had been half-ruined buildings everywhere around this district, thanks to flying bombs that had fallen off course, but she was much too young and the experience of being in a place like this was probably novel to her.

At length he said, "Would you mind if we did ask around after her, though?"

"All right," she consented without enthusiasm. "But suppose she just ran off in fright and—well—fell over the cliff there, perhaps?"

"We'll have to bear that in mind too," he agreed, and took her hand to lead her out.

By the door he stopped. He had at first not noticed, because of the drifting ash that covered almost everything, but now he caught a sudden glimpse of brightness on the floor. Stooping, he brushed away ash from a broken mirror. There was a nail-hole in the wall where it had hung.

"Knocked it down in her fright at the fire," he said. "I suppose . . ."

IX

RORY DUNSTABLE LEANED over the stern of the pirate radio ship and watched his fishing line unreel into the water for the umpty-dozenth time since he came out after lunch. Overhead, the black flag with the white skull-and-crossbones symbolizing defiance of radio regulations fluttered limply atop the two-hundred-foot mast mounted on the converted coaster from which they operated.

It was a fine, calm, and extremely dull day. If it stayed like this over the weekend, there would probably be several boatloads of fans rowing or chugging out from shore to call on the ship and be shown round, perhaps interviewed on the air if any of them seemed interesting enough. But today things were very quiet, and after doing last night's midnight-to-three show he had time on his hands until 6 P.M.

He was a good-looking young man, smart in a stretch toweling sweater with the skull-and-crossbones embroidered on the chest, and a pair of immaculately creased yellow pants. He was stretching his lunch-time beer to its utmost—the proprietors would not allow the disc jockeys to drink except at meals, for fear of something disastrous happening during a broadcast—but it was becoming warm and flat now.

Everyone else who wasn't working, including the two other DJ's, lay sunning on the foredeck. But he liked fishing over the stern in calm weather, regardless of catching anything. It allowed him to run over and over in his mind the gimmicky, wise-cracking presentation of his next stint at the mike.

Apart from a ship heading for London, and the launch from the marine research station which usually put out two or three times a day to measure water temperature and current velocities, there was nothing in sight on the level water, unless you included the seaside resort towns to the north and south, just visible through the clear sunlit air. He sighed and gulped down the last of his beer.

At the same moment there came a tug on the line. He exclaimed and hauled on it, realizing the moment he took a grip that he had hooked something enormous that was fighting back.

He shouted for help, wrapping the line tight around his hand and bracing his elbows on the rail. Soon the other two off-duty DJ's—plump Gerry Furnival and wiry little Mitch Porter—came running along the deck.

"Christ, from the way you were howling I thought you'd fallen overboard!" Mitch said in mock dismay. "And here you still are!"

"Can it and give me a hand!" Rory panted.

"Isn't your line going to break if we try and haul it aboard?" Gerry demanded.

"If it breaks it breaks, but this is the biggest damned thing I ever hooked! Shark or something, maybe! Somebody get my camera just in case I do lose it at the last moment!"

"You fishermen," Mitch muttered with a shrug. "Okay, Gerry, you help him and I'll fetch the camera. And maybe something to gaff it with—isn't that the term?"

"It's weakening!" Rory snapped. "Gerry, grab hold and pull—but don't jerk!"

A short eternity of a few minutes passed while the two of them gradually eased the line in. It could be felt that the violent tugs from the prey were diminishing as it tired. From somewhere inship, the monitor speaker said in the cheerful tones of Hank Lorton, the duty DJ, "Chum Rory seems to have caught a whopper astern there—the place is in turmoil what with people getting cameras and things! I'll let you know. . . ." And a door shut off the sound before the next record started.

Six or seven more people—the maintenance engineers, technicians, and other staff—assembled to watch the final moments of the drama. Mitch had found the movie camera and was adjusting it for light-level as the first sign of the catch showed through the blurring water.

"*Shark?*" he said in a puzzled tone as he focused on it. The motor began to run with a faint buzzing noise.

"No, it's not a shark," Rory said. "But what is it?"

And then, for one brief instant, the thing showed above the surface. They saw clearly, as though the bright summer sun had frozen the outline during its brief visit to the upper air, a sleek fish's body—and then there was *not* a fish's body, but something that could thrash the water into spray with many more appendages than simply fins and a tail. The spray doused them and they flinched back, although Mitch kept gallantly on filming.

"Pull, Gerry!" Rory shouted. They heaved together, and for a second heartbeat of time they saw the thing, this time completely clear of the water.

And it was not a fish. It was a squid, with flailing tentacles and—

"Christ, it's got a tail," Rory said. "But squid don't have—"

Snap.

The line parted, and the thing, whatever it was, dropped back into the sea and was gone.

There was a moment of complete astonished silence. At last Gerry said, "Octopus?"

64

"Not octopus—squid." Rory stared at the fading patch of bubbles. "But squid don't have tails like that!"

Mitch shut off the camera and clapped him jovially on the shoulder.

"Never mind, baby!" he said. "Here's more proof than fishermen generally get, in this movie film!"

"Yes," Rory said thoughtfully. "Yes, I think I'm going to want that film."

It was a very depressed group of singers and musicians who arrived at the Mellow Cellar that evening. Even Rupert White, the fourth instrumentalist, had seen the piece in the morning paper and called Bruno after jumping to the obvious conclusion, and Bruno was in a foul temper when Dick Marvell, the chairman of the management committee, greeted him.

"Well, you got fuzz crawling out the walls yet?" he snapped.

"Bruno, I'm sorry," Dick said in a placatory tone, mournful-faced under his Jesus-like brown hair. "But if even Monty—"

"Yeah, even Monty," Bruno said, and pushed past carrying his electric bass.

In the cramped dressing room he parked it and moved to the only chair not loaded with gear belonging to the Sceneshifters, the other group sharing the premidnight bill with them at today's session, whose thunderously amplified lineup of three guitars and drums was making the walls shiver. He began to lay out his props: masks, hats, and enormous fingerless gauntlets of shimmering aluminum foil.

"Dick says it's a packed house again," Gideon reported, moving in to join him.

"So?" Bruno grunted, and there was a miserable silence while the rest of them came in and made ready for their first set. Liz, in a hip-length dress of five layers of contrasting colored nets over orange tights, didn't need to make any more preparations, but sat in the corner watching the others.

"Bruno, it's not like the end of the world," she said finally.

"It's not me I'm worried about," Bruno snapped. "Or us! But it might have been the end of the world as far as that cat on the beach was concerned, hm?"

He lifted his bass out of its case. Silently the others copied him: Gideon with his guitar and Rupert with his collection of miscellaneous instruments including such exotica as Swanee whistles and a Jew's harp. His regular instrument was the electric organ, but that was already delivered and on-stage, like Glenn's drum kit.

Shortly, Dick Marvell put his head around the door. "We're going to play two tracks from the new Stones LP, okay?" he said. "Then you're on. Stage B, same as last time."

"What's coming after?" Gideon called as he made to leave.

"Oh, some poetry with jazz—Sally French and Mick Conti. And a sort of half-assed happening is fixed for 1 A.M., that Rupert knows about."

Rupert bridled. He was the most talented of the group, they all agreed to that—he had studied at the Royal College of Music and come away with a first-rate result. But he found his own talent boring; he played nineteen instruments competently, from harmonica to bagpipes, and lately he had been concentrating on the electronic effects he could wheedle out of a tape recorder with a score of curious attachments of his own design. Some of the items he had come up with were strangely disturbing, but so far the group had not found a way to integrate the latest of his discoveries into their stage performances, only into their records.

Enormously tall, with a wild crown of bright red hair, he was even more of a crowd-puller than Gideon with his witty, pointed, sometimes savage lyrics, and what he himself always called his built-in appeal to liberal thinkers— to wit, his West Indian descent.

"Save it for later," Bruno said to him, seeing that he was all set for an argument with Dick. "Let's go, hm?"

The Mellow Cellar was the converted basement of a warehouse, which had been in its time the site for jazz clubs, skiffle clubs, an unsuccessful strip club, and this latest project, a "total environment" with light projectors, film clips, and pop groups alternating throughout twelve-hour sessions once a week from 8 P.M. to 8 A.M. It was proving fantastically profitable, but what the Hermetic Tradition chiefly appreciated was the quality of the audience. Prepared to listen to ragas, jazz, pop, and poetry in the same context, they offered the chance to try out the wildest of Rupert's experiments. On their last visit they had brought his homemade Lasry-Bachet organ, a contraption of glass rods played with a wet finger, and tonight they were going to try some masked numbers, with dialogues between Gideon and Liz spoken over the rhythmic background of their regular instruments. Rupert had declared that *Sprechgesang* was as yet hardly exploited.

During the playing of the record, many of the audience had drifted to the soft-drink and snack bars. Bruno called *Seadeath*, which because it had made the Top Twenty, even if only for two weeks, was their best-known number and would remind the listeners who they were. Shimmering silvery chords like the rippling of calm water came from Rupert's organ, and the boom of his own bass chimed in like the footsteps of approaching doom. Gideon moved to the center mike and started to declaim his lyric, with Liz at the side mike whispering a countermelody. With brushes, Glenn underscored the clashes between the two opposing themes.

On the floor, barely half the audience were dancing. Most of them were standing and swaying, watching the play of greenish light that the projectors flooded over the stage. Since they had done most of their numbers on previous visits, Bruno had only needed to hand a set of cue cards to the man running the lights tonight; they would do their big experimental item to a film clip Rupert had located.

But for the first set: mostly conventional stuff, apart from props like the glittering gauntlets he wore for his own featured number, *Nighthound*, when the special attachments Rupert had designed for his bass made the strings roar like demented lions and the audience shuddered at every vast welkin-smashing chord.

He was beginning to relax into the familiar context of the music, forgetting the annoyances of the day and looking forward to the conceit-breeding—but welcome—applause that would end their set, when Dick caught his eye and moved toward the stage on which they stood. At the conclusion of the number he beckoned Bruno to him, and whispered.

"What did I tell you? Fuzz we got. Some busy called Sergeant Branksome, all the way from where you were last night. You can see him in my office after the set. But for Chrissake lose him as fast as you can!"

X

THERE WERE TWO people waiting in Dick's office when Bruno entered, scowling, at the end of the group's set: Sergeant Branksome, looking even wearier than last night, and a young man in a dark suit who introduced himself as Sergeant Jenkins of Scotland Yard. Branksome had moved off his own patch by coming up to London; he would naturally have had to ask permission of the Metropolitan CID, Bruno realized.

He threw himself down into a chair facing the policemen over Dick's desk, took out a cigarette without offering the packet, and said shortly, "Well—what is it?"

"Did you meet an old lady called Miss Beeding last night on the way to your beach party?" Branksome said without preamble.

"Yes, she stopped us and spoke to us. We gave her one of the bottles of beer we had with us and she went away happy."

"And that's all?"

"Of course."

"I see." Idly, Branksome looked down at the phone on the desk and moved a fingertip around the dial, his nail clicking on the holes. "Did you go to her house, or any of your group?"

"Christ, no. Actually she said it was in a mess so she couldn't invite us for a cuppa, but it looked pretty much of a ruin and we were damned glad she didn't latch on to us." Bruno hesitated. "Why, what's happened?"

"We don't know," Branksome admitted. "But Constable Sellers went to her house today, and found signs of a small fire, from a smashed oil lamp. And *no* sign of Miss Beeding. I had people out checking the neighborhood all afternoon. So I thought I'd better call on you and find out what you knew about her."

"Think we made away with her or something?" Bruno snapped.

"You're very edgy, aren't you, sir?" Sergeant Jenkins put in with just a hint of a sneer.

Bruno brought himself up short. "I'm sorry," he said unwillingly. "I've had a very bad day thanks to a paragraph in this morning's papers, which I suspect is the fault of your Mr. Warden, sergeant!"

Branksome had the grace to look a trifle embarrassed. He said, "Yes, as a matter of fact I told him off about that."

"Thanks," Bruno grunted. "But I imagine he just laughed."

"More or less, I'm afraid—" Branksome shrugged. "But in answer to your question of a moment back: no, I don't think you or your group—what was your term?— 'made away with' Miss Beeding. There's a considerably more likely angle. You reported that the man you claimed to have seen coming up from the sea behaved very oddly, didn't you?"

Bruno nodded warily.

"Did he strike you, or offer you any violence?"

"Well . . ." Bruno sighed. "All right, I might as well come out with it. I didn't tell you this last night because I was bloody well ashamed of myself. But he behaved so strangely that—well, we panicked. That's why we didn't manage to bring him along with us, and maybe get him to a hospital. He looked horrible, like I told you, with his face all eaten away. But what got us was the way he acted."

"Would you say in lay terms that he appeared to be out of his rational mind?"

"I guess I would," Bruno agreed. "He didn't seem to want to be helped out of the water, though he was wringing wet and very cold. Then when we saw his face we—we panicked like I just said. But Gideon kept his head and persuaded us to go back and help him. And he wasn't there any more. There were just some tracks leading off along the beach that eventually ran into the water."

He leaned forward. "Do you think he could have been dangerously crazy, and done something to the old woman?"

"It seems possible," Branksome conceded. "That's why I'm following the matter up. Would you mind if I spoke to the other members of your group, without you talking to them first?"

"Of course not," Bruno muttered. "Though, like I said, you may find they're a bit ashamed of admitting we got scared and ran off when we realized how horrible he was."

Nodding, Branksome turned to Jenkins. "Could you find the manager and get him to send another of the group in?" he requested.

"Get Gideon Hard and Glenn Salmon," Bruno said. "Rupert White didn't come with us yesterday—he was working in town."

"Sellers said you had some girls with you," Branksome said. "Are they here tonight?"

"Liz Howell sings with the group," Bruno said. "She was with us. And my girl-friend's here too, dancing on the floor somewhere, I guess."

"Well, I don't imagine we'll need to hear from everyone," Branksome shrugged. "Thank you, Mr. Twentyman."

Bruno rose and headed for the door. On the threshold he paused. "You haven't had a report of an escaped maniac, have you?" he demanded.

Branksome shook his head.

"Have you thought of finding out whether anyone fell overboard from a passing ship? He was terribly wet—he was saturated with water, so much that he was incredibly heavy to lift to his feet."

"Thank you, sir," Jenkins said sarcastically. "We don't really need to be told how to do our own job, you know."

Bruno glared at him and went out.

His job was making Roger Sellers prematurely cynical. When, after failing to find anyone near the old Warrinder farm who had seen Miss Beeding recently, he phoned in to his station and reported her absence, he was fully expecting Doreen to complain about the way he was neglecting her in favor of his job even though he was off-duty, and make her way back to town to find another of her boy-friends who was less involved with his work and had more time to spare for her.

Somewhat to his surprise, she said suddenly, "It is like you see on the pictures and the telly, isn't it?"

"How do you mean?" he countered, puzzled.

"Well, like you always have to be ready to do things to help other people even if you're not officially working." She gazed at him with a thoughtful expression.

Sellers hesitated. He said finally, "Well, I don't know if it sounds soppy, but that's the bit about the job I like. Most of it is pretty dreadful—chasing people who parked in the wrong place, or nicking some half-witted old dear for shoplifting! But—well, this part of it sort of makes up for the rest, you know?"

She nodded.

"Want to stick around?" he suggested, and after a moment she nodded again.

So she hung on the fringe of events as first a car from the local fire station, then a police car carrying Sergeant Branksome, arrived at the gateway beside the lane. The fire officer inspected the filthy farm kitchen with a knowledgeable air, poked into corners to make sure there was no further danger, and departed. Meantime Branksome investigated the odds and ends he found lying about, and eventually said with a puzzled frown, "See anything odd here, Rodge?"

"There's *something*," Sellers agreed. "But the place is in such a mess anyway. . . . Wait a moment. I get you. There was a struggle?"

"I think there may have been," Branksome said. "It's not just the broken mirror. There's a broken beer bottle here, see?" He turned over crumbling ash from a sheet of burned paper with his toe, and there were the bright splinters on the floor. "And the door, too."

Sellers stared at it. It was half-twisted off its top hinge.

"And nobody nearby recalls seeing her today?" Branksome pursued.

"No, sarge. I spoke to everyone I could find."

"In that case," Branksome muttered, "maybe there really was a man who came out of the sea."

He pulled his overtired self together, straightening to his full height as though he had just realized he was stooping.

"We'll have to start a search," he said.

It was very late in the evening when Sellers managed to get away and take his bird for a bite to eat in Brindown's only late-night restaurant—Chinese, like a great many such in contemporary England. Doreen was very excited by the day's events, and chattered merrily on while he reconsidered the drawbacks of his job when it came down to finding and keeping a girl-friend.

Along about half-past ten, when on a fine summer night like this one the pubs turned out not just a few late-staying customers but a good crowd of people who had decided it was too early to go home before they had to leave, they returned to the street and set off toward the car-park where he had left his scooter.

Arm in arm, picking their way through the other people heading the same way, or the opposite way to catch the last buses out to the surrounding villages, they strolled without haste and occasionally grinned at each other.

But abruptly Sellers stopped dead in his tracks.

"There she is!" he burst out.

"What?" Doreen demanded.

"Didn't you see—? Oh, no, you don't know her, do you? I just saw Miss Beeding, there ahead on the other side of the junction. Come on!"

He seized her hand and hurried her forward. But when they came to the next corner, there was a shrill hoot and a car thrust ahead of them, almost bumping his legs. He glowered at the driver, who merely stared back, and by the time the car had passed, there was a fresh group of people clustered on the other curb, leaving another pub.

They pushed through them, but the street beyond was empty and there was no sign of Miss Beeding.

"Damn," Sellers muttered. "But I'm certain I saw her. She's absolutely unmistakable! She only has one set of clothes, a horrible ragged old skirt and a kind of cardigan thing. . . . Doreen, do you mind very much if we pop in the station on the way to your home and tell them that she's been seen?"

"Of course not," Doreen said. "I didn't know about her. I think it's awful that people still have to live the way she does!"

Tonight's duty at the station was being taken by one of the other three young constables, Marty Swires. But when they entered, rather puffed from their hurry, they found he was not alone. Sergeant Branksome, as they knew, had gone off to London to see if he could get any further news of the mysterious stranger from the sea out of the members of the Hermetic Tradition, but talking to Swires across the inquiry desk was a portly man holding a hat and with a coat slung over his arm as though on the point of leaving.

Recognizing him as one of the senior detectives who had come out from county headquarters when Branksome put out his search call, Sellers shook his hand free of Doreen's and drew himself up to an official stance.

"Excuse me, sir—Chief Inspector Neville, isn't it?"

Nodding, the portly detective turned.

"Oh, yes, of course," he said. "You're the man who started us looking for the crazy old woman, aren't you? Saw you earlier on. Well, we found her all right, and she is apparently disturbed."

Sellers felt a moment of absolute blankness. He said uncertainly, "But it can only just have happened. I came in to say I spotted her in the High Street"—he glanced at the clock—"about ten minutes ago."

Neville shrugged. "You must have been mistaken," he said. "She was found wandering over toward Geddesley at about nine, and she's in the mental hospital there. Has been for well over an hour."

"But I tell you I saw her, sir!" Sellers took a pace forward. "We have her in here regularly on Saturday nights, when she's got herself a bit merry. I should know!"

Neville frowned at him. "Yes, constable," he agreed bitingly. "You should know, shouldn't you? But obviously you don't. I tell you she's been confirmed as the person who was brought into Geddesley Mental Hospital well over an hour ago, and that's that—the job's finished and I can finally get home. After all, there can't very well be *two* old women answering precisely the same description around here. Can there?"

"But I saw her as plainly as I see you!" Sellers insisted.

"Then I'd recommend a good oculist," Neville snapped, and made for the door. "Good night!"

XI

"MORNING, SARGE," SELLERS said as Branksome came into the police station.

"Morning," Branksome grunted. "I hear my trip to London was wasted after all—that right?"

Sellers hesitated. He said after a moment, "That does seem to be the case, sarge. Except—"

"Except what? Miss Beeding's safely locked up in the bin at Geddesley—that's what they told me, anyway."

"Yes, but—" Sellers looked extremely unhappy. "Well, it was like this, you see. You know the Chinese restaurant in the High Street? I took Doreen there for a meal last night, and round about half-past ten, when the pubs were turning out, we were walking back to the car park in Hook and Line Street. We were on the corner opposite the Ring of Bells when—well, I could *swear* I saw Miss Beeding in among the customers coming from the saloon bar there. We were held up by a car when we tried to cross over, and when we got to the other side there was no trace of her, but I thought I ought to come along here and report seeing her. And that was how I heard that she'd already been found. Chief Inspector Neville was here and said she'd been located more than an hour earlier, over Geddesley way."

He looked hurt. "But I'd know her anywhere, sarge. I mean, I've helped put her away on Saturday night dozens of times!"

Branksome wiped his face; the day was starting very warm again.

"What do they say at Geddesley?" he demanded.

"I tried the hospital directly I came in, but I couldn't get the doctor in charge, so I had to leave a message, and apparently nobody's been up to the hospital from Geddesley police station yet, but they promised to get someone along as soon as they could to question Miss Beeding."

"Have they found out yet whether she claims to have been assaulted by anyone?"

"The sister I spoke to at the hospital said not—it was the first thing I thought of, because of course if she was attacked by the man Bruno saw come out of the sea, he may turn on someone else."

"Of course," Branksome echoed ironically. "I take it she answers to the right name, though?"

Sellers stared down at the polished surface of the inquiry desk.

"I asked that, too," he muttered. "And they said yes, she says she's Miss Beeding all right."

Heaving a sigh, he added, "So I *must* have been mistaken. Honestly, though, I saw her as clear as I see you. I just can't figure it out!"

"You want to watch that," Branksome said caustically. "Or you'll wind up where she's been taken, won't you? Leave it to the Geddesley force, hm? At least she's moved off our patch for the time being, and that's a relief. Things are busy enough here during the holiday season without having extra problems dumped in our laps."

But, as he continued toward his office, he added over his shoulder, "Let me know directly the Geddesley people call in, won't you? If she was attacked by this man, and didn't simply run off in panic when she broke her oil lamp, we'll have to start a search for him right away."

Except in very rough weather—when the people on board lived off the supplies that were kept in deep-freeze throughout the winter—the converted coaster that had been turned into Radio Jolly Roger was served three times a week by a boat that came out from a small fishing port nearby with mail, supplies, and rotating personnel, particularly relief DJ's, who spent one week in four ashore doing publicity and compèring dances and pop shows sponsored by the station. Rory Dunstable was just finishing breakfast when the chug of the boat's engine came through the open portholes.

He was in a very gloomy mood, not so much because he had yesterday lost the biggest fish he had ever hooked but because the others were continually making gibes about "the one that got away," which were good-natured enough but with repetition had become unendurable.

Suddenly he thrust back his chair. "For the Lord's sake!" he exploded at Mitch, who had just made yet another crack on the same subject. "Can't you get it through your thick head that I'm *not* setting myself up to be the world's great expert on fish? All I'm saying is that that thing didn't look or act like any fish I've ever heard of. You were there on the deck at the time—Christ, you were actually filming it! Didn't it look peculiar to you?"

"All right, so you hooked a coelacanth or something," Mitch shrugged. "For me, fish is what comes wrapped in batter with a portion of chips and a shake of vinegar."

Hank, the DJ who had been on duty at the mike when the fish was hooked, said in a placatory tone, "Look, Rory, you have pictures of this thing, haven't you?"

"Provided Mitch worked the camera properly," Rory snapped.

"So if you're so worried, why don't you have the film developed and show it to the people at that marine research place just along the coast?" Hank suggested.

"Exactly what I had in mind myself," Rory said grimly. He swigged the last of his coffee, wiped his lip, and tossed his napkin on the table. "I'll send it ashore with the supplies boat and tell them to have it processed as quickly as possible."

He spun on his heel and marched out. The others exchanged amused glances.

"I think he's really narked because he couldn't bring it on board and get it stuffed and hung up in a glass case," Mitch said. "I didn't know he took his fishing so seriously. I always thought he just did it to pass the time."

Much later in the day, Sellers put his head around the door of Branksome's office. The sergeant looked up with a scowl.

"Sorry, sarge," Sellers muttered. "But Geddesley just came through about Miss Beeding, and—well, it all sounds very weird to me. I think you'd better talk to them."

"All right, switch it through," Branksome sighed, picking up his own phone.

Shortly, a voice said, "Constable Crick, sergeant! I'm speaking from Dr. Nimms's office at Geddesley Mental Hospital. I gather this old lady who was brought in here last night after being found wandering lives over your way and you know her pretty well, is that right?"

"Yes."

"Well, Dr. Nimms seems to think there's something very odd about her. Not just the kind of behavior you might expect from a batty old dear, which is what she looks like, but—well, it's all too technical for me, I'm afraid. Perhaps you'd have a word with him yourself."

There came the sound of the phone being passed from hand to hand. Then, in brisk professional tones: "Sergeant, this Miss Beeding of yours—have you ever known her to be violent?"

"Violent?" Branksome echoed in surprise. "Lord, no! Anyhow, she's too skinny to be violent—no more strength than a sick puppy. She doesn't eat properly, and she's just a bag of bones."

"Hmmm!" A faint rasping, as though the doctor was scratching an unshaven chin. "Well, that certainly doesn't sound like the woman we've got here, to start with! She was found last night wandering in a dazed condition, I'm told, and didn't give any trouble at first. But after she'd been delivered here by ambulance and put in one of the security cells we reserve for undiagnosed patients, she turned nasty on my staff. She's filthy, of course, and the nurse on duty was going to strip and wash her, and—well, she says she couldn't. Didn't dare lay a hand on her. The old woman gave her a nasty bang on the cheek—I saw the bruise this morning. And considering the state she's in, she's remarkably strong. I've had a go at her myself, and she broke my grip on her without the least difficulty."

"This is ridiculous!" Branksome said.

"Ridiculous or not, it's what's been happening," Nimms asserted. "She's all right so long as you don't try to touch her, I find. I've been able to carry out one or two tests on her, for example, and it was the result of these that made me suggest to the constable here that he get in touch with you."

"What do you find so strange?" Branksome demanded.

"Well, if I had to put a name to her condition, I'd say she's suffering some sort of partial amnesia. She appears to know her name all right—she answered the first of my questions about that—but there are . . . I suppose you might say there are lacunae in her memory. We had food taken in to her, for example, and she refused it, so the nurse tried to coax her a bit—no, let me correct that. She

81

didn't refuse it, she ignored it. So the nurse tried to persuade her, saying things like 'Don't you like carrots?' and such. And apparently she just stared at the carrots, although she identified the meat all right, saying it was beef, which it was. And then—"

"That doesn't sound very odd to me," Branksome interrupted.

"It's only an untechnical example," Nimms said. "I could give you some more technical ones if you want. I've just been to see her and given her an association test which is standard for patients suspected of senile dementia, and she seemed to answer about half of it correctly and the rest she simply ignored as though she hadn't heard the questions. But there's no pattern in her refusals to answer. Normally there are particular areas of experience that are affected by amnesia, especially recent experiences which have been suppressed owing to shock and so forth. But I can't find any consistency here whatever. And another thing. Didn't you just say she was a skinny thing, very thin and weak?"

"Ever since I've known her," Branksome agreed.

"That's *very* funny," Nimms said. "I'd have said she was—not exactly fat, but certainly plump. I felt her arm when I was trying to get hold of her, and she was by no means bony."

He hesitated. During the momentary pause, Branksome's memory threw up the recollection of what Sellers had said, in such an injured tone, about seeing her in Brindown High Street last night.

"Do you think you could possibly come over, or send someone, to identify her positively?" Nimms said. "There does seem to be a discrepancy here, and I'd like to sort it out before taking any further action."

"Yes, I'll send one of my men over—it's not very far," Branksome answered after a further hesitation. "As a matter of fact, I was going to ask you something else, which I don't think ought to be left until somebody from here can get to you. Did you manage to question her about the reason why she was wandering about?"

"I did my best to get some sense out of her on the subject," Nimms said. "But she's very confused indeed, you know. All I could establish was that she was on a beach or something and she met someone, but according to the constable here she was supposed to have been assaulted, and she didn't react at all to the relevant questions. I rather gathered that she merely talked to the person she met and then went off."

"What we're actually afraid of is that she may have been attacked by someone who was reported to be behaving in a strange fashion quite close to her home," Branksome explained. "But if she doesn't claim to have been attacked, that's that, I suppose. Did she say anything about a fire?"

"No, we haven't had anything out of her on that score, I can tell you definitely. Directly the constable mentioned that there had been a fire at her home, I asked her about it, and the response was nil."

Branksome sighed. "Well, that's as much as we can hope to sort out over the phone," he said. "I'll try and get someone who knows her over to see you during the afternoon, if that's okay."

"More than okay," Nimms said in a grim tone. "I think it's indispensable."

XII

THE RIDE FROM Brindown to Geddesley was a pleasant one, especially at this time of year—mostly along a winding country road between hedges heavy with their full summer greenery, occasionally meeting tourists and holiday-makers from the local caravan sites or visiting the Roman remains on the coast.

Zooming along on his scooter, however, Roger Sellers was in no mood to enjoy it. He was badly worried by the events of the past twenty-four hours, regardless of whether they made sense—and what he had overheard of the conversation between the sergeant and Dr. Nimms suggested that as yet they didn't.

Even when they did fall into a sane pattern, though, he felt they wouldn't be very pleasant. He had not been very long in the police force, and up until now most of his time had been occupied with what he had described to Doreen: chasing motorists who parked in the wrong place and nicking old ladies accused of shoplifting.

Today, however, there was the scent of the first real mystery he had encountered in the air. Already, when all that could definitely be said to have happened was that Miss Beeding had disappeared, he had begun to worry a little; later, when it became clear that she might have been assaulted, he worried more. Now, when he was on his way to prove to himself that she was actually in hospital as Chief Inspector Neville had assured him, he felt badly disturbed.

"Hell, I did see her in Brindown!" he said to the air. He swerved the scooter around the last bend before the road he was following brought him out on to a major highway, and had to brake abruptly as a large tanker truck, presumably bound for the Organic Acids depot, loomed ahead of him.

But how—the train of his thoughts resumed as the huge vehicle squeezed by—could one account for things like the doctor at the hospital calling Miss Beeding "plump"? She was skinnier than a rat, and always had been!

"There she is," Dr. Nimms said, and slid back the inspection hatch in the door of the small cell to which Miss Beeding had been assigned. He was a tall, bluff man of early middle age, wearing a lightweight summer suit that contrasted alarmingly with the clothes of the patients Sellers had seen on his way through the wards. They were in shabby much-washed garments of cheap cotton, few of them retaining their own clothing, and almost all of them seemed to be displaying an identical expression of misery which matched his own gray thoughts, bar a few who had grinned at him with idiotic unaccountable happiness. The hospital was an oppressive place, and he hoped to be out of it quickly.

He obediently set his eyes to the inspection hatch, and started.

The room beyond—too small to be called a room, in fact, but holding a few items of furniture, a bed, a locker, and a chair—was crudely painted in pale yellow with many scrawled names and obscene remarks on its walls. Its only window was head-high and barred on the outside. Under it, between the bed's head and the right-hand wall, a figure stood whom he could clearly see.

A sort of Miss Beeding. But ...

He took a deep breath. As Dr. Nimms had stated, this

woman was far from scrawny. Her limbs, where they emerged from the grayish blur of her clothing, were almost puffy; her face was slack-skinned, her cheeks drooping strangely to obscure the sharp line of her jaw. Her eyes were round and blank, and her forehead, which he recalled as being heavily lined, was smoother than a baby's.

"It looks like Miss Beeding," he said at length, in a doubtful tone.

"What do you mean, 'looks like' her?" Nimms challenged.

"She looks fatter somehow," Sellers said. "I don't understand this at all."

"Well, there are conditions which can rapidly generate surplus fat, but they don't take place overnight," Nimms said shortly, "We'd better go in, hadn't we, and see how she reacts to someone she knows? You do know her, I believe?"

"Slightly," Sellers agreed. "She always seems to have enough money to get a bit tight on Saturdays, and we almost always have to put her up for the night. Her old age pension, I suppose."

He stood back while Nimms unlocked the door and, plucking up his courage, accompanied him into the cell.

Miss Beeding (*was* it Miss Beeding? But who else could it be?) stood immobile in the corner under the window, regarding the intruders with suspicious blank eyes. Dr. Nimms addressed her in a soothing tone.

"Here's somebody you know, Miss Beeding!" he said. "He's from Brindown, isn't he, where you come from?"

She made no response. Sellers studied her, better able to inspect her face and clothing from inside the door, and a faint tremor went down his spine as he started to spot differences almost too vague to describe, yet impossible to ignore. Ever since the first time he had seen her, he had always recognized her as much by her clothing as by her features: that horrible grease-shiny skirt dangling close to her ankles, which had originally been navy blue and was now a kind of off-blue-gray-black, and the buttonless cardigan, which in winter was covered by a torn brown tweed coat and a coarse woollen scarf.

It wasn't so much that the shape of the clothing was wrong—the skirt drooped to the right level on the legs, the cardigan bulged and sagged more or less as usual.

But the texture, somehow . . .

He reached out unconsciously to touch her arm, and she slammed at him viciously, almost karate-style, missing his wrist by a fraction as he jerked out of reach.

Summoning all his self-control, he spoke in the same soothing tone as Nimms.

"Miss Beeding! You know me, don't you—Constable Sellers?"

The slack mouth worked and after a while sounds emerged from it.

"You're the new young at Brindown," she said distinctly. "There in the where I go on Saturday because the won't leave me alone."

He blinked at her, puzzled; then he glanced at Nimms in the hope of an explanation.

"She's been talking like that since she was brought in, apparently," Nimms said under his breath, and himself addressed her.

"Where is the place they send you to on Saturdays, Miss Beeding?"

She grimaced at him. "In the there is the young—this one, him!"

"It's extraordinary," Nimms muttered. "You see, constable, what I can't account for is the way she composes her statements. You just heard a couple of examples, didn't you? As though some of the words are being left out without her noticing. Now amnesia usually relates to some identifiable experience, generally a shock, and that part of the memory is as it were temporarily blanked out. But I've never known a condition where words get left out in the middle of sentences! Whole blocks of referents, yes; single words, no!"

He shrugged and turned to go. Glad to be out of the cell, Sellers passed him and waited for him to relock the door.

Outside, he said, "What are you going to do with her?"

"I'm not sure. We'll have to try and make her cooperate, naturally—those clothes look revolting! So far she hasn't eaten anything; perhaps she'll accept her supper and show signs of cooperation afterward. If she doesn't, we'll have to do something I personally detest, and that is force her. If a day's starvation weakens her enough, we can give her an injection in the morning, and relax her enough to get her stripped and washed and so on. Beyond that—"

Suddenly he broke off. "This *is* your Miss Beeding, isn't it?" he snapped.

Sellers, taken aback, shrugged. He said, "Well, sir, if I saw her on the street I'd think hello, that's old Miss Beeding, and then I might go up to her and accost her, and when she turned around I'd think Lord, I've made a mistake. And I can't put my finger on the way I find her different. But she *is*."

"Fatter, as you said?" Nimms rapped.

"Yes, but that's not all. I've always seen her in those same old clothes, for well over a year now—since I joined the force at Brindown. And they looked different just now. Slicker. Greasier. Smoother, if you follow me." He said this with a dogged air, as though prepared to be told he was talking rubbish.

"Well, she answers to the right name," Nimms said

caustically. "So we'll have to assume this is the right person, won't we?"

"Of course," Sellers muttered, and walked toward the exit.

Bruno had called a rehearsal of the group this afternoon at the request of Rupert, who had a new effect he wanted to try out, and Gideon, who had come up with a set of lyrics he wanted to have set to music. They rehearsed in his apartment, which he owed to his family's generosity and which was much bigger than the homes of the other members of the band. He had sometimes thought that he could ascribe his nominal leadership of the Hermetic Tradition as much to that as to his ability as an organizer; Monty Krein was their business brain, not Bruno.

Around 3 P.M. they began to trickle in with their instruments; Glenn was the first to arrive, yelling for someone to haul his drum kit up the stairs. Helping him with the bulky equipment, Bruno saw a door on the landing above his open, reveal a scowling face, and close again; his neighbors upstairs had small reason to love him because of the rehearsals in spite of their attempts to keep noise down. But renting rehearsal rooms was ridiculous, and they all disliked rehearsing in empty club rooms because the absence of the audience affected the impact of the sounds they made.

"Where's Cress?" Glenn panted as he deposited the bass drum and hi-hat cymbal in the middle of Bruno's living room.

"Cress is working on a private project," Bruno told him. "It's more than my life is worth to interrupt her when she's painting or modeling."

Gideon arrived in the doorway, brandishing not only his guitar case but the stands for Glenn's other cymbals, and reported having seen Rupert's mini-van draw up across the road. After another ten busy minutes they had everything installed and were connecting up the amplifiers, adjusting the volume to the lowest level possible without distorting the frequency response, when the door from the room which Cress used as a studio slammed wide open and they whirled.

Staring at them was a figure in black sweater and tight black pants whose face was eaten away from cheekbone to jawbone, the image of the man they had helped out of the sea at that beach in Kent.

Gideon exhaled sharply. "Cress!" he exploded. "What's the idea of that, for Chrissake?"

Cress removed the mask she had covered her face with, to reveal an expression of such seriousness that the rest of them were struck silent.

"Is it a likeness?" she said after a pause, regarding the mask critically; it was made of buckram soaked with glue, shaped, painted, and built up with ordinary plasticine.

"It's the spitting bloody image," Bruno said.

"I thought so," Cress said. "But . . . Here, look at this, will you?"

In the hand not grasping the mask she held out a folded newspaper. The others crowded to examine it. It was dated Tuesday of the current week, the day after the test pilot had crashed off the Kent coast, and prominently displayed a photo of him.

"That's where I took the face from," Cress said. "And I put the bare bones and teeth on it. And it's a perfect likeness, you say. Do you see what that means?"

"It means—" Bruno said, and had no chance to finish before she interrupted him.

"It means that the man we saw come up the beach *was* the missing pilot, exactly as that bastard reporter claimed!"

XIII

Worried, and much depressed at his own inability to figure out what could explain the curious wrongness of the Miss Beeding he had seen at the mental hospital, Sellers made the sharp turn from the main Geddesley road into the winding lane that would lead him back to Brindown. A short distance beyond, he passed the gate of the Organic Acids depot, beyond which loomed the tall cylindrical tanks and complex webs of piping that stored and delivered the firm's products. They apparently needed vast quantities of cooling water for the processes they employed, and had been given a shore site because the commercial demand for what they made—bulk chemicals of a type that might otherwise have to be imported—was regarded as much more important than the complaints of local residents.

"Hey! Hey, officer!" A voice hailed him as he rode by.

Braking carefully, swinging around, Sellers found that the person who had called to him was a lean man of early middle age, wearing a dark suit and striped tie, who had been speaking to the gatekeeper through the window of the latter's small timber hut.

"Yes, sir!" he said as he pulled to a halt level with the gate.

"Good afternoon," the man said. "Sorry to stop you like this, but—well, I'm Graham Fleet, and I'm the assistant managing director, and I've just heard something from Murphy, our gatekeeper there, which I was about to call and let you know about."

"Yes, sir?" Sellers said, affecting an air of polite interest.

Fleet swallowed hard. He said after a pause, "There may not be anything in it, of course—"

"We're always pleased to have suspicious events reported by the public," Sellers said, consciously quoting Sergeant Branksome.

"Yes. Well!" Fleet mopped his face with a handkerchief from his breast pocket, thrust it back, and spoke rapidly. "Apparently someone has been seen prowling around our depot here, and nobody's been able to catch up with her."

"Her?" Sellers echoed.

"Yes. An old woman, so Murphy says. Murphy!" he shouted suddenly. "Come on over here and tell the constable what you heard."

The gatekeeper, an elderly man in a brown suit, came out of his hut and approached. "Well, officer!" he said. "We've had three reports so far today—one from a lorry driver who brought a tanker in, two from our own staff— that some old woman has been seen wandering around the waterside terminal, where the barges dock with the raw materials. Very shabby, they said—dirty old clothes. But spry. One of them went after her and just couldn't catch her up."

Sellers felt a dizzying spasm of disorientation, as though the world had slipped off its axis. He said, "When was this?"

"First one was about lunch-time," Murphy said. "Then the other two were after lunch—the latest an hour or so ago."

"We have some very poisonous chemicals here," Fleet said. "We have 'no trespassing' signs up, and there are always night patrols to stop holiday-makers wandering off the beach on to our territory, but—well, there is a limit to what one can do, isn't there?" he concluded in an exasperated tone.

"I was wondering if maybe it was the old lady who lives in the tumbledown house a mile or two along towards Brindown," Murphy offered.

"No, it can't be her." Sellers spoke with an assurance he did not feel. "She's been taken to hospital. Look, sir, I think you should call my sergeant at Brindown 230 and tell him about this. Unless you want me to come in right away and mount a search for her . . . ?"

Fleet shook his head. "We can't spare the time today," he muttered. "I have thirty thousand gallons of chemicals due by sea and road before quitting time, and some of them are late already. Very well, I'll phone the station as you suggest. Sorry to have stopped you."

"That's all right, sir." Sellers kicked his scooter back into life and rode away down the narrow road.

But all the time it took him to regain the police station was spent in thinking: *It can't be, it can't be, it CAN'T be!*

"That's that, then," Tom Reedwall said, raising the latest of the day's sampling containers over the stern of the research station's little launch *Morrhua*. He decanted the contents into a plastic jar, labeled it with the date, exact time of day, and location, and dropped it into the rack in the well of the boat. "All right, Sam, let's head for home."

At the wheel, Sam Fletcher shrugged and started the motor again. Over its rising racket, he shouted, "Get anything on the crashed plane, did you?"

Tom scowled at the back of the other man's head. Even without Sam Fletcher's irritating attentions to his wife Netta, he didn't think he would have liked the man—he was too greasy, or in the standard slang word, "smarmy." His last remark could on the face of it have been a tribute

93

to Tom's suggestion that if the missing aircraft which had crashed near here on Monday last had gone to the bottom with a full load of fuel, their regular water samples might reveal traces of it and so help to identify the exact spot where the wreckage lay.

Somehow, though, the tone in which it was delivered excluded all possibility of approval. . . .

But he called back, politely, "No, I don't think so—though I'll have to wait for the analysis, of course."

After that there was silence between them as the launch chugged back toward the research station. The purpose of these twice-daily trips was to map the exact temperature and pollution levels along the North Kent coast, with an eye to the eventual establishment of sea farms breeding edible fish within easy reach of London's teeming millions. Already the government had leased a few patches of beach where oysters—bred from the famous "Whitstable native" strain—had been established on wire-strung frames developed by the Japanese, to keep the spat clear of predators on the bottom of the sea, but so far the contaminated water had kept down the crop. Hereabouts, it wasn't only that London sewage and that from other nearby cities helped to poison the water; various chemical factories and refineries, especially the big Organic Acids depot, caused additional trouble, and the fish, which might have coped with ordinary biological wastes, proved too sickly in face of industrial ones.

Reedwall sighed. He had taken up his job in the ambitious hope of making some sort of contribution to the problem of overpopulation and famine, by improving the yield the sea offered to the fisherman. So far, he felt he had spent more time in sorting out administrative difficulties than in actually advancing the cause he believed in.

His eyes roamed the adjacent coastline, picturing in imagination the time, very soon expected, when London's sprawling bulk would have absorbed even this area into its colossal urban mass, and suddenly stiffened.

"Hello!" he exclaimed. "Sam, look over there—look at the Organic Acids wharf! Isn't someone waving to us?"

Fletcher turned his head. He was especially handsome in profile, and knew it. There was no doubt of his cleverness, or his talent for the job he had taken on, but Tom did often wish that he could sometimes betray a hint of interest in someone else besides Sam Fletcher.

"I'll put about," he said, and suited the action to the word. Shortly, the launch bobbed in toward the concrete wharf, flanked by storage tanks and set about with pumps and valved pipes, through which Organic Acids received most of its bulk consignments. Under a wooden frame holding a board with the company's name on it, a man Tom recognized was waving to them.

"Mr. Fleet!" he acknowledged, rising in the stern of the launch and calling loudly over the engine's noise. "What is it?"

"Can I ask you a favor?" Fleet said apologetically. "Keep an eye on the foreshore as you go back to your base, will you? We've had reports that an old lady has been seen around our storage tanks, and she might get hurt."

Tom started. He said, "What—a shabby old woman with gray hair, her skirt right down to her ankles?"

"That sounds like her!" Fleet stared at him. "Have you seen her around?"

"No, I thought it might be Miss Beeding, who lives in the burned-out farm over there." Tom waved in a generally eastward direction.

"Oh, it can't be *her*. I just spoke to a policeman who told me she's gone to hospital," Fleet said with relief. "But there must be more than one crazy old woman in the world. Keep an eye out, there's a good fellow, and let the police know if you spot her!"

Tom shrugged and glanced at Sam Fletcher, who smiled automatically and put the launch about toward the sea again.

Moved by a sudden impulse, when he passed the lane leading from the road toward the marine research station, Sellers swung around and drove down it. He came to the gate at the bottom, let himself through, and cautiously picked a more or less level course for the scooter along the rough track beyond. When he came to the first of the buildings, he got off and looked around curiously. He had never visited the research station before. But it was much as he had imagined from the sight of other government foundations: the buildings designed to keep costs down, constructed from the cheapest kind of plain concrete, roofed with corrugated iron or prefabricated slabs.

"Oh, hello, constable—can I help you?"

A pleasant female voice startled him as he was gazing about. He turned to find a girl with sleek fair hair, wearing a white lab coat, carrying a fine-mesh net in one hand and a sample jar with a tight stopper in the other.

"Good afternoon, ma'am," he said. "Ah—routine inquiry! Are you on the staff here?"

"I'm Dr. Reedwall—Dr. Netta Reedwall, that is. My husband is out in the station launch on a sampling trip, I'm afraid. But I think Dr. Innis is in his office; that's the director, if you want to see him . . . ?"

"Well, frankly, ma'am, I just dropped in on the off-chance. Have you, or has anybody else, seen an old lady wandering about the foreshore recently?"

"I certainly haven't, and I'm sure my husband would have mentioned her if he had." Netta hesitated. "Not Miss Beeding, you don't mean?"

"That's right, ma'am."

"No, I'm sure we haven't. I think we all know her by sight at least. Why, has something happened to her?"

Sellers shrugged. "Possibly," he said, mind working furiously. "She's had to be taken to hospital, you see, and we would like to know if anyone noticed her behaving oddly."

"Oh, the poor old thing!" Netta exclaimed. "Well, I'll certainly ask if anyone saw her come by here."

"Thank you." Sellers hesitated. "By the way, ma'am, how many people work here?"

"Well!" Netta shook back her hair. "If you mean permanent staff, there's just Dr. Innis, Dr. Fletcher, my husband and myself, and our two maintenance technicians. But up to last week we had nearly sixty people on the site. We had some new fish pens put in because we're hoping to get some dolphins, and we had all the workmen coming and going." She hesitated. "Why do you ask?" she added at length, looking puzzled.

"Simple curiosity, ma'am," Sellers said with a grin. "We're always supposed to familiarize ourselves with the district we work in."

She laughed. "Well, any time you want to know more, just drop in, won't you?"

XIV

As HE HEARD the sound of the *Morrhua*'s engine approaching, Inkosi raised his head. He was lying in the shadow of the incubation house, the long, low building where experimental batches of fish spawn and oyster spat were being raised under ideal conditions, away from the predators that would have devoured them in the wild water of the sea.

The moment the launch bobbed in to her mooring, he let go a loud bark and hurled himself across the wharf.

"Get that bloody animal of yours away from here!" Fletcher shouted, flinching back as though afraid the dog would charge him and knock him overboard.

"For heaven's sake, Sam!" Tom snapped at him. "He's never tried to jump into the launch yet, has he?"

"There's always a first time," Fletcher muttered as he stepped ashore with the painter. The door of the incubation house opened, and two figures emerged: Netta first, then, a pace behind, Dr. Innis, the director of the station, a white-haired man with a perpetually harassed air, as though unable to forget that this, like all the similar projects he had been associated with before, was a poor orphan when it came to allotting government expenditure for the year.

Sam Fletcher dropped his voice and spoke viciously to Tom out of the corner of his mouth.

"One of these days that damned dog *is* going to jump

on board, you know, and probably smash the day's sample jars with those bloody great paws of his!"

"Oh, stuff it!" Tom said tiredly, and climbed on the wharf to greet Inkosi. The dog responded with a woof of delight and a threshing of his tail.

"Dr. Reedwall!" Dr. Innis came hurrying down the wharf agitatedly. On the point of hoisting up the crate of sample containers, Tom checked and glanced around.

"Yes, sir?"

"Someone's been prowling around the incubation rooms!"

"Prowling around? How do you know?"

"I went to make the regular afternoon tests and measurements," Netta said. "And I found every last one of the doors in there had been opened. I'm dead certain I closed them when I left this morning."

"Probably that dog," Fletcher muttered, making the last turn around the bollard to which the *Morrhua* was moored and moving to join the others.

"This wasn't anything a dog could do," Innis said sharply, to forestall the renewal of a familiar argument between Fletcher and the Reedwalls. "Those doors don't have handles a paw could push down—they're fitted with knobs, and you'd need hands to turn them with."

Fletcher shrugged and looked superciliously at the Ridgeback. He had no time for pets of any sort.

"Is there any damage?" Tom demanded.

"Not that we can see," Netta reassured him. "But nobody ought to have been in there at all today, not since I did the morning tests. We've talked to the technicians and they both swear blind they haven't been in."

"We were wondering about one of the workmen who were here last week," Dr. Innis said. "Do you remember the one who said he loved oysters so much he'd sell his soul for a dozen of them?"

"Him?" Tom laughed scornfully. "That was a joke, sir! Certainly I remember him—Paddy Ryan was the name, I think. But he wasn't so silly as to imagine he could grow his own oysters in a tank at home, was he?"

"Well, we can't think of anyone else who might have been messing around in here," Dr. Innis sighed.

Tom snapped his fingers. "Sam! Remember what that man at the chemical factory said to us just now?"

"About the old woman?" Fletcher said, and explained when Tom gave a nod.

"That's funny!" Netta exclaimed. "There was a policeman here a short while ago, while you were out in the launch, saying she'd been taken to hospital—Miss Beeding, that is—and he asked me to find out if anyone had seen her around here."

"Well, there's your answer, then," Fletcher shrugged, and bent to pick up the crate of water samples. "Come on, Tom, we have to see to this lot before we leave tonight, and—"

"Not so fast," Tom objected. "Sam, you can't have been listening. Mr. Fleet at the chemical depot said he'd been told it couldn't be her, don't you remember?"

"That was the woman who's been seen wandering around their place, not around here," Fletcher grunted. "As far as I'm concerned she can sabotage the entire installation they have—it'd stop them fouling the water, anyhow!"

"I don't think I quite follow that," Dr. Innis said after a puzzled pause.

"What Sam means," Tom amplified, "is that there must presumably be two batty old ladies wandering around. I think it's pretty unlikely myself. If the police said Miss Beeding is in hospital, the poor old so-and-so can't very well be held responsible for what happens here or at the Organic Acids plant, can she?"

Dr. Innis sighed. "I can't fathom this," he said finally. "But it doesn't matter, I suppose. Since no harm has been done, we'd better forget about it. Carry on with your work, but keep an eye out for anyone hanging around here, won't you?"

"I simply can't make head or tail of it," Roger Sellers said in an aggrieved tone.

"What?" Doreen demanded. They were sitting opposite each other in Brindown's only coffee bar, very crowded tonight with people who had come down from London to spend the weekend.

"Well, whichever way you add up this funny business about Miss Beeding, it doesn't make sense." He drew a deep breath. "Look, first of all she vanishes, right? From her home. We find traces of a fire at the farmhouse, and then we find signs of a struggle. Then we see her right here in Brindown—"

Someone had put a coin in the jukebox; he was cut short by the loud blaring of a Pet Clark disc. Doreen seized the chance to interrupt him.

"I didn't see her, Rodge!" she objected. "I wouldn't know her if I did."

"All right, *I* saw her!"

"But the inspector said you couldn't have," Doreen insisted with maddening female logic.

"Blazes, he hadn't been to the hospital, had he? I have!" Sellers sipped his coffee. "And the more I think about what I saw there, the more I feel it wasn't Miss Beeding who was locked up in that cell!"

"So who else could it have been?"

"Goodness knows—I don't. But—well, look." He leaned forward earnestly. "Imagine you knew someone who was sort of famous. Imagine there was a play about him on the telly, or a picture was made about him, and they went to a lot of trouble to get it all exactly the way it really happened, do you follow me? Wouldn't you know, by looking at the actor who was pretending to be this person, that it wasn't the same man?"

"Yes, I suppose I would," Doreen conceded after a moment for thought.

"Well, that's exactly how I felt when I saw Miss Beeding in the hospital," Sellers declared.

"But what reason could anyone possibly have for pretending to be Miss Beeding?"

"That's what I haven't yet figured out," he sighed. "But that's not the whole of it, you see. Today, on my way back from Geddesley, this Mr. Fleet at the chemical works tells me three different people have reported an old woman wandering around their—what did he call it?—their seaside terminal, I think he said. That must be the bit you can see from the water, with the pipelines and tanks."

He almost bit at his coffee with exasperation. "Goodness, 'Reen! There aren't *that* many old women wandering around here, are there?"

"I don't know, and I don't think I really care," Doreen said after a pause.

"Come off it! Weren't you saying yesterday that you thought it was a good thing for me to try and help people and worry about them even if I wasn't on duty?" Sellers spoke in an injured tone.

"Yes, but that's not quite the same as what you're doing this evening, is it?" Doreen said. "I mean, you aren't making sense, are you? I don't believe in there being two Miss Beedings."

He stared at her. "I wasn't trying to—" he began, and broke off in confusion.

"That's what I make out of it," she said. "You're trying to say there are two of them, one in hospital and one at the chemical works. Far as I'm concerned, people only see double when they're squiffy, and there's got to be some other explanation, which will probably be perfectly ordinary when you get to it."

Depressed, he stared down into his cup, which now held only dregs. Doreen started to gather her belongings.

"I think you'd better take me home," she said.

Having dropped her off, Sellers was waiting at a stoplight on his own way home when a car drew up alongside and a voice hailed him.

"Evening, *constable*!"

There was no mistaking that sarcastic voice. "Evening, *Mr. Leigh-Warden*," he muttered, doing his best to match it.

"I hear you were at the marine research station today," the reporter said with a grin.

"How the—?"

"Oh, I have my contacts!" Leigh-Warden chuckled. "If you're going to amount to anything in your job, you'd better take a leaf out of my book, hadn't you?"

Sellers could only stare for a moment. While he was sitting dumbly astride his machine, the lights began to change.

"I'll pull up across the road," Leigh-Warden told him. "Want to have a word with you, as it happens!"

Annoyed with himself at being persuaded to stop and talk, Sellers followed the car over the junction. When it was possible to draw in to the curb, Leigh-Warden did so, and got out. Sellers, remaining on his scooter, looked at him.

"Tell me in confidence," he said in a conspiratorial voice, "is there or isn't there something funny going on?"

"I don't think I quite understand," Sellers muttered.

"Don't try to pull wool over *my* eyes, young feller-me-lad!" Leigh-Warden said sharply. "I'm nearly old enough to be your grandfather—in fact for all I know I am, because I was a pretty wild chap when I was your age! And I make my living by sniffing out scandals."

"I know!" Sellers said, nettled. "Holiday wife-trading and things like that," he added, using the example he had quoted to Bruno and the Hermetic Tradition.

Leigh-Warden smiled. "Don't think you can get under my guard with anything as crude as that! People like to read about that sort of thing and so papers will buy the odd story along those lines, and that's how I make a living. It could rub off on you, you know."

"You know what you make it sound like?" Sellers said. "You know that stuff they put on money they think is going to be stolen? The chemical that turns blue or green and you can't wash it off?" He scowled. "I'd rather have clean hands, myself!"

For a long moment Leigh-Warden stared at him. The stare turned into a glower. Without another word he spun on his heel and got back into his car.

Feeling partly proud of himself, partly as though he had just behaved like a fool, Sellers engaged gear on his scooter again and shot away up the street.

XV

LEIGH-WARDEN ROLLED his car up the short drive-way of the bungalow where he lived on the outskirts of Brin-down, gravel crunching under the wheels, switched off, and got out. Without bothering to open the garage and put the car away, he went indoors. He poured himself a nightcap and sat down in an armchair, his expression thoughtful.

He had no particular illusions about himself. He could have been—should have been—a staff reporter with one of the mass-circulation London daily or Sunday papers, instead of a freelance eking out a precarious living in a backwater provincial district. Somehow, one by one, chances he should have seized had slipped away from him, and he had started to drink too much, and time passed, and eventually he had been forced to admit that he could look forward to only one kind of future: identical with the present.

Nonetheless he had always had a nose for news. Much of the time it was wasted on spotting clues to petty scandals. Sellers had just gibed at him for making his living off things like holiday wife-trading, and that was by and large the truth. The sensational weeklies always liked that kind of story, and paid well for the full juicy details. He kept himself informed about other subjects, too—whatever was making headlines. If one of the nationals showed interest in bad maintenance of long-distance transport, he had a local story to send them the following day; if there was a question in parliament about sewage pollution on Britain's beaches, he had interviews with caravan users ready to print.

Pop groups were nowadays always good for a short item and sometimes a major story, which was why he had been able to tell Bruno and Sellers that he did watch "Top of the Pops" on television. He kept in touch with everything that bred news.

But out of that chance encounter and what had happened subsequently he could feel a pattern emerging. He didn't yet know what it might be, but he was confident enough of his own judgment to gamble a lot of time and trouble on following it through. He had spoken to Sam Fletcher at the marine research institute; he had called at Organic Acids; he had tapped every resource of his own personal grapevine.

And—he gave a pleased nod—the pattern was continuing to grow.

Pounding back down the dark ribbon of the M1 motorway from a dance in Birmingham, the Hermetic Tradition spoke little to each other. It was late and they were all tired.

When they did speak, however, the same subject seemed to recur and recur—the alarming mystery Cress had uncovered. Taped to the van's dashboard, mutely reminding them every time they glanced at it, was the mask she had made: the face that was a ruined version of the missing test pilot's.

"But what can have happened to him?" Bruno said aloud, not expecting an answer.

Behind him, Gideon sighed. "He probably wandered back in the sea, man!" he exclaimed. "They'll find him washed up on the Dutch coast next winter, maybe!"

"Yes, but this old woman ran off, didn't she—like she was scared? And now she's in a mental home and—"

"She could have been put away any time in the past several years, surely," Liz objected. "Maybe she should have been. Living alone in a burnt-out house like she was!"

"People are too damned ready to shove other people in asylums," Glenn grunted. "I think it's a good thing she was allowed to live the way she wanted." He hunched around on the seat. "By the way, I was saying to Bruno at the interval back there: I think we ought to go ahead and try and fix this beach session whatever the hell Monty says. Gid, what do you think?"

"I think maybe we should pick another site," Gideon answered. "I don't imagine they like us too well down that way."

"I'm inclined to agree with Glenn," Bruno said. "Sort of on principle. I think we should go back as soon as we can and find out if we can get permission from whoever owns the land."

"You're wishing headaches on yourself," Gideon sighed. "But okay, I won't try and stop you."

The night watchman at the Organic Acids depot switched off the big flashlight he carried as he entered the brightly lit gatekeeper's hut. He had made two rounds of the entire plant so far tonight, without spotting any sign of the old woman he had been warned about. Whoever might have been wandering around during the day seemed to have gone.

He turned on the electric boiling-ring and went to fill his kettle. It was time for a midnight cup of tea.

Outside, under the quiet stars, the huge black tanks and intertwined piping of the plant were silent, stiff as a petrified forest beside the rippling sea.

Alone in the home that once had been shared, Sergeant Branksome lay sleepless in spite of exhaustion, staring at the ceiling of his bedroom. He was haunted by visions of old Miss Beeding. Sometimes he thought that was how he might wind up himself—dirty, irrational, alive but without any reason to go on living.

The duty male nurse at the Geddesley Mental Hospital peered through the hatch in the door of the cell where Miss Beeding was confined. She was still standing in the corner, as she had been all day, close to the window.

The nurse hesitated. He was an idealistic young man, not very long in his job. It seemed to him a terrible thing that she should stand like that all night, when she ought to lie down and rest her old bones. Perhaps if she were spoken to kindly, persuaded . . . ? After all, it must be a terrifying experience to be whipped away from her familiar background and suddenly locked away in a strange place among people she must recognize as insane.

After a moment's consideration, he checked the ring of keys he carried, located the right one, and opened the door.

Entering, he said in a soothing voice, "Come on, dearie! Why don't you lie down and get some rest, hm? You can't just stand there the whole night long, can you? You—"

In a mental hospital, screams at night are commonplace events.

"I'm going to bed, darling," Netta Reedwall said, closing the book she had been reading and getting out of her chair. "You?"

Tom hesitated. He said, "I don't think I could sleep. I don't know why, but my mind's buzzing. I think I'll take

Inkosi for a trot along the beach first, and see if I can relax."

"What's making you so restless?" Netta said. "I've noticed—you've been on edge all evening."

Tom shook his head. "I can't put my finger on it. Maybe it's that business in the incubation building."

"Yes, that was odd." Netta frowned. "The most sensible explanation was Doc Innis's—the laborer who was here who said he liked oysters so much. And that is definitely absurd, isn't it?"

"Of course it is," Tom shrugged. "I thought old Paddy was much the nicest of the people we had working here, not like one or two of the others. You heard that a couple of them got in a fight in a pub and wound up in court, didn't you?"

"No, I didn't hear about that."

"I think Sam Fletcher told me."

"Well, I don't talk to *him* any more than the job requires," Netta said tartly. "There's something about him that makes my skin crawl, honestly!"

Tom got to his feet and caressed her hair affectionately. "That's a relief, anyway. I think I might be worried if you liked him."

"It's no good you trying to be jealous," Netta smiled. "You haven't got the temperament for it. Or the excuse. All right—enjoy your walk and don't be too long."

At the word "walk" Inkosi, who was drowsing in a corner, cocked his head alertly and gave a soft encouraging growl, a kind of question: *Did I hear that right?*

"Okay, boy," Tom said with a chuckle. "Come on, let's go and see if we can start a few rabbits, shall we?"

With a frantic wag of his tail Inkosi leapt up and dashed to find his lead, returning with it in his mouth and almost grinning with eagerness.

At the microphone of Radio Jolly Roger, Rory Dunstable settled himself in his chair.

"Good night and good morning to all you late-and-earlies," he said in his professionally ingratiating voice. "This is Mister Rory, famed in song and story, taking over the hot seat at your favorite pirate station from now until three ack-emma with music for the quiet hours. For the last time in some while, by the way—I go ashore tomorrow for a short holiday which I think is well deserved, but there are those who don't agree with me and I *hate* them. . . . Coming back from a stint on hard dry land is Hugo Masterson, and he will be offering his own special blend of disc and voice as of—let's see now—yes, the noon-to-three show tomorrow, *pree*-cisely twelve hours hence. Meantime, though, here's me and here are the *Jefferson Airplane!*"

He hit the switch that started the tapes rolling, leaned back, and frowned at the sky visible through the porthole.

The night was still and warm. The moon had been up earlier, but had now set; nonetheless the sky was bright—a thin overcast caught the gleam of London's lights and smeared it out over half the heavens. Tom turned in the Geddesley direction, the one in which he could walk less far because his way along the shore would be blocked by the Organic Acids depot.

For a while he strolled slowly along, with Inkosi darting from side to side of him, now dashing to the sea's edge to sniff the scent of the tide, now heading madly inland to inspect some randomly-chosen tuft of grass or the base of a tree.

His mind continued to whirl like a motor, as though he had taken amphetamine, and he began to grow angry with himself. All he wanted to do tonight was sleep. The weekend was ahead of him, and he didn't have to work in the morning; he had hoped, though, to get up early and go skin diving with Netta. This was not a very rewarding area for divers, but he wanted to keep in practice because they planned to go diving in the Mediterranean at the end of the summer.

He was walking randomly, hardly thinking of where he was going, when all of a sudden a sound came out of the night that made him stop dead.

It was the sound of a man crying.

A woman or child crying out here on the lonely shore would have been bad enough, but the noise of a man weeping is far more terrifying. He ran forward in the direction from which it came, shouting, and almost at once he encountered two people staggering up from the beach: the weeping man, and—clinging to him and sobbing herself—a woman in her late thirties who might have been pretty, but whose face now was a mask of fear.

"Good God!" Tom exclaimed. "Paddy Ryan—?"

Inkosi danced up out of the darkness, sensed something was wrong, and sat down with a puzzled expression, panting loudly.

"It's Dr. Reedwall," the man said between whimpers. "Oh, Jesus and Mary, Jesus and Mary! Look, will yez? Look at this, and it's an old woman that done it, a simple little old woman weak as my own baby daughter. *Look!*"

He thrust his right arm forward, and Tom had to struggle against the urge to vomit. The arm was there. But the hand was not. From the wrist down, there was nothing but a stump smeared with blood that seemed black as the pitch of hell in the twilight.

"An old woman," Ryan said again. "Mother of God, I'd swear to it on my father's bones, an old woman looking harmless as you please!"

111

XVI

Furious at being dragged out of bed at this time of the night, Chief Inspector Neville swung his car off the main road and down the winding lane toward Brindown. He raced past the dark silent skeleton of the Organic Acids plant and, a few hundred yards beyond, had to brake sharply. Ahead of him was an ambulance, the blue light on top flashing brilliantly, stopped while the driver talked to a constable in shirtsleeves.

Neville backed his car, ran it far enough on the verge to let the ambulance pass when it left the spot, and got out. As he approached the constable on foot, the latter called to him.

"Chief Inspector! Thank God you got here!"

"Oh, yes!" Neville said. "It's Sellers, isn't it? We met the other day. *Now* what's all this nonsense?"

In the glare of the ambulance's lights, Sellers's face was almost greenish, and contorted with incipient nausea. "Not such nonsense, sir," he muttered. "Go and look for yourself."

He pointed through a gap in the hedgerow, on the side toward the sea, and, turning, Neville saw lights beyond, and figures moving. Another moment, and two uniformed ambulance attendants appeared in the opening, helping a man whose face was perfectly white.

But it was not his face which appalled Neville. It was the fact that his right arm ended at the wrist in a blunt stub covered with bandages.

"Who's here?" Neville demanded harshly of Sellers. "Who's in charge?"

"Sergeant Branksome, sir," Sellers said, and had to swallow hard. "And Dr. Reedwall from the marine research station, I think, and—and this man's girl-friend."

Neville stared at the injured man as he was helped into the ambulance, and made as though to address him, but one of the attendants guiding the casualty shook his head.

"He's not in a fit state to answer questions, sir," he muttered. "Lost a lot of blood. Shocked, of course."

"Why isn't he on a stretcher, then?" Neville countered.

"Won't have it, sir. We tried, but he's still strong and we couldn't force him."

"Who is he?" Neville asked.

"Name's Paddy Ryan, I think, sir," the attendant said, and, in answer to a call from the driver, added, "Right away, Jack! Just let me climb aboard!"

As soon as the rear door was shut, the driver started to seesaw back and forth, turning around in the narrow lane. Neville didn't wait, but climbed through the gap in the hedge and called Branksome's name.

Shortly the sergeant appeared, waving a flashlight. He had not stopped to dress properly, but had come out in a sweater and slacks over his pajamas. "Good to see you, sir," he said. "This is a terrible thing, isn't it?"

"I still don't know exactly what's happened," Neville said.

"We got the call from the marine research station about half an hour ago," Branksome said. "That man you just saw being taken away—he was found by Dr. Reedwall wandering along here. He had a woman with him, a Mrs. Spicer. She's over there, being looked after by Dr. Reedwall's wife. Apparently—no, maybe you'd better talk to her yourself. This way."

Neville followed, glancing about him as he went. It

looked as though Branksome had handled the situation competently, he decided. There were at least a dozen men in view wielding torches and carrying out a meticulous search of the area—everyone, presumably, who had come in answer to the emergency call.

Not far away, sitting on the ground wrapped in a blanket, was a woman whose teeth chattered uncontrollably, and whose eyes were staring blankly into nowhere. Beside her, a pretty girl in a dressing gown and sandals was pouring hot tea from a thermos flask and trying to persuade her to drink it. Neville indicated to Branksome that he should wait a moment; then, when the frightened woman had managed to gulp down a little of the tea, he said, "Mrs. Spicer? I'm Chief Inspector Neville. Can you tell me exactly what happened?"

The woman said in a moaning voice, "It's not right, it's not fair—Paddy's such a nice fellow! And how will he get his living with only one hand?"

"Here!" the girl in the dressing gown said, and made her take a little more tea.

"What happened to his hand?" Neville asked Branksome softly. "Looked as though it had been chopped off!"

"Not chopped so much as *digested*," Branksome answered equally quietly. "As though he'd dipped it in acid!"

Neville gave him a blank stare and addressed Mrs. Spicer again. This time she passed a weary hand over her face and managed a coherent answer.

"I'm divorced, see, and all on my own. And Paddy come down here to work on the thing at the marine station there—big new concrete tanks, he said. And we got talking in the pub the first night he was here, and tomorrow he's off to look for another job so we decided we'd come out here to be alone for a bit—we weren't doing no harm to anybody! And all of a sudden we hear someone coming, and he jumps up, and there's this funny little old woman, so he says good evening to her politely enough, and she puts out her hand, and he does the same because he was a bit merry, you know? And suddenly he shouts out. He shouts, 'Mother of God, it burns, it burns!' And when he pulled free he hadn't got his hand any longer. Oh, God, it was awful, it was awful. . . ."

She put her head in both hands and leaned forward, rocking and crying. The girl in the dressing gown looked up at Neville as she put a comforting arm around her.

"Don't bother her with any more questions, inspector!" she said. "She's in a terrible state. Ask my husband if you want any more details."

"No sign of anybody, sergeant!" a voice called, and Tom emerged from the darkness, carrying a flashlight. He gave his wife a quick smile.

"I was just telling the chief inspector here how you put in the emergency call," Branksome said.

"Yes, that's right. I was walking the dog before going to bed. I've had him with me all along the beach for at least half a mile, but he didn't seem to scent anything." He snapped his fingers. "Inkosi! Come here! Sit—good boy!"

Inkosi, looking very pleased at the big adventure he was caught up in, obeyed and sat with his tongue hanging out at Tom's side.

Neville hesitated. He said after a pause, "Sergeant, you mentioned that Ryan's hand looked as if he'd dipped it in acid, didn't you?"

"That's what it reminded me of," Branksome nodded.

"Could that in fact be what he did?" Neville suggested. "There's a lot of acid there at the chemical works, isn't there?"

"No!" A cry from Mrs. Spicer. "I tell you it was an old woman that did it!"

"That's obvious nonsense," Neville murmured, giving Mrs. Spicer a reassuring false smile. "But I imagine our next step is to search the chemical plant for traces of an intruder, don't you think so?"

"Inspector, that's a long way from here for a man who's just lost a hand!" Tom objected. "He'd have fainted from the shock and the loss of blood, wouldn't he?" Checking, he glanced at Branksome.

"Is something wrong, sergeant?"

Branksome was looking alarmed. He said, "Sir, do you remember my telling you about the man who was reported on the beach the other night by members of the pop group who had a picnic near here?"

"Yes, of course," Neville agreed.

"Well, sir, he must have lost a lot of blood too, if he was injured in the way they described to me. I don't suppose it's more than a coincidence, though."

"I don't see how there could be a connection," Neville said shortly. "Frankly I find it impossible to believe in some old woman who dissolves a man's hand with acid, don't you? There was one old woman around here, but she's safely tucked away in hospital—right?"

"Constable Sellers—" Branksome began.

"What about him?"

"Well, sir, he—he says he's none too sure the woman in the hospital *is* Miss Beeding. I told him he was being stupid, but he's stuck to his story. Also he said he saw her the other night when according to you she was already in the hospital, isn't that right?"

Neville shrugged. "Well, the sensible thing at the moment seems to be to find out what Ryan did to his hand— Hello! What's that commotion over there?"

Out of the darkness from the direction of the beach two men came running and shouting. "Sarge!" the first one called. "We spotted somebody! We went right along almost to the chemical works, and there was someone, and it looked like the old woman!"

"But that's ridiculous," Neville said slowly.

"We didn't get a clear look at her, sir," the man said, "but we caught a glimpse, and that's what it looked like."

"Heading for the chemical works?" Branksome rapped.

"Looked like it, Sarge!"

"We'd better go that way, then. Sir, I know it *sounds* ridiculous," he added to Neville, "but Dr. Reedwall here knows Ryan—met him while he was working on the dolphin pens at the research station—and he says he's reliable."

"Yes, definitely," Tom declared. "Isn't that right, Netta?"

"He seemed very nice and very sensible," his wife agreed. "I can't imagine him dreaming up a story like this!"

"What I can't imagine," Neville said grimly, "is a story like this making sense! But—all right, let's move in that direction, then. Sergeant, put in a call for search equipment, will you? See if you can get some floodlights, to start with, and ask the coast guard if they can send a launch along to watch the seashore."

"Right away, sir," Branksome agreed.

The night watchman at the Organic Acids plant moved off on the latest of his regular tours of the grounds. He was getting rather tired now, but he had still some six or more hours before the daytime gatekeeper turned up to relieve him. With the circle of brightness from his torch going ahead of him like a firefly, he moved between the fences of piping that connected the tanks.

Suddenly he checked. Ahead, coming toward him from the wharf at which the barges docked to deliver their raw materials, he had seen a shadowy figure.

"Hey!" he called out, and hurried forward, taking a fresh grip on the truncheon that was his only weapon. He was not a young man, and running was difficult for him, but he had no trouble in catching up with the intruder, who stood still as though waiting for him.

Puzzled, he saw by the light of the torch that it was an elderly woman, very shabby. He said uncertainly, "What the—?"

And she lunged at him. He cried out and raised his truncheon, jumping away from her, thinking she must be crazy. She came after him, hands raised like claws, and made a second grab. This time she managed to catch his sleeve. The cloth tore, and for an instant he felt a burning sensation. He yelled, and this time—in pure reflex—used the truncheon. It landed on her right arm with a smacking noise.

Her grip broke. Turning tail, he doubled for the safety of the gatehouse, where there were bright lights and the cheerful music from Radio Jolly Roger. He dashed inside, slammed the door, and picked up the phone.

"Police, quick!" he shouted to the operator who answered his call. "There's a crazy old—"

Checking, he turned to the window. Outside there was a noise of engines. Cars with blue lights on top were pulling up before the gate.

"It's all right," he said rather foolishly to the phone. "They're here. Lord knows why, but they're here!"

XVII

"WHAT DO YOU make of it?" Tom said, as he and Netta returned arm in arm toward their home. A police car had taken Mrs. Spicer away, and the men who had come to scour the area had moved away to the east; whatever they might be searching for, amateurs were likely to be more of a hindrance than a help from now on.

Netta shivered. "I don't know. But it must have been awful."

"It was—believe me." Tom's tone was somber. "I never saw anything so horrible as that poor devil's arm, not cut off clean, which might not have been so bad, but just . . . Well, raw!"

"An acid-thrower?" Netta suggested.

"There's no kind of acid that could dissolve a whole hand in a few seconds. You'd need fluorine, or something of that order. And throwing it or spraying it wouldn't work quickly enough. You'd have to immerse the whole hand and keep it there somehow."

"It's fantastic!" Netta said.

"Gruesome," Tom muttered, and whistled Inkosi to follow them as the welcoming lights of their bungalow appeared ahead. "You were wonderful, by the way," he added. "Thanks for turning out so promptly."

"I'm glad we could be of help." Netta paused at the door and waited for him to find his key. "That poor woman must have suffered nearly as much as Paddy did.

Don't let anything like that happen to you, will you, darling?"

"Over my dead body," Tom said with cynical mock-cheerfulness, and let her into the house.

"Let me get this straight!" Neville said to the night watchman. "You saw someone, Mr. Hedges, and you went to see who it was. You found this old woman and she attacked you."

"It sounds daft," the night watchman said apologetically. "But look here, at my sleeve—see?"

Branksome peered at the torn fabric, bent close, and sniffed. He said, "Sir, that's been burned with acid! Notice the brown marks on the shirt underneath? And how red the skin is turning?"

Puzzled, Neville copied the sergeant and after a moment nodded. "It looks as if you're right," he admitted. "So we have an acid-thrower, do we? I don't much reckon sending men after one of them in the dark!"

"We got protective clothing!" Hedges offered. "I have keys for everything here, see?" He held up a jingling ring of them. "There's these suits the men wear when they're handling corrosive compounds, see? Though I suppose I ought to get permission to send them out."

"Can you reach someone?" Neville snapped.

"Well, it's Mr. Fleet's pigeon because he's in charge of deliveries and transfers. . . ." Hedges looked thoughtful. "Yes, I think I have his phone number."

"Ring him up right away, tell him what's happened and say we need to use his protective clothing in case this crazy old bag throws acid at some of our officers. Quick! And give the keys to Constable Sellers—we don't want to waste any time."

"That's the one," Hedges said, complying and selecting one of the keys. "The suits are kept in the hut down the drive on the left, the one marked 'Protective Garb.' You'll spot it easily enough."

Sellers seized the keys and hurried away.

Inside the hut Hedges had sent him to, he found hanging on wall-pegs half a dozen outfits of impervious plastic, each with gauntlets and a masklike helmet with wide flaps at front and rear to cover the wearer's neck. He issued them to the first of the men who had come after him, and retained the last for himself. Struggling into it, except for the helmet, he made his way back with his companions to the gatekeeper's hut.

"Mr. Fleet's on his way!" Hedges announced as he came in earshot. "Says it's all right to use the suits. He'll be about ten minutes."

"Can you give us some light?" Neville demanded over his shoulder, inspecting the men who had put the suits on with a look of approval.

"Yes, sir!" Hedges moved to the back of the hut and pushed over a large switch from "Summer" to "Winter." Then he started to flip down a series of smaller switches, and the entire area of the chemical plant was suddenly transformed into a wonderland of brilliance. On every storage tank, at every road intersection, and over the main door of every administrative building, lamps sprang to life.

"Branksome!" Neville said. "Take three men in suits and half the ones without, and fan out to the east side, all right? I'll take the rest of them and work the west side. Hedges, you stay here, and when Mr. Fleet turns up let him know what we're doing. Tell him to come and join me, but to be careful to stay in the middle of the roadway and not go along any dark shortcuts between the buildings —is that clear?"

"Right, sir!" Hedges said crisply.

"Let's move, then," Neville said, and went out of the hut.

Vaguely regretting that he had appropriated one of the protective suits for himself—because without it he would have been in the rearguard, not the vanguard, of the searchers—Sellers moved uncertainly down the main roadway toward the easterly end of the chemical firm's land. Behind him followed two constables from a county headquarters car that had answered Dr. Reedwall's original alarm call, both in the acid-proof suits with gauntlets and helmets, and behind them again came Branksome and a couple more constables without protective garments.

The chemical works was an eerie place by night, he found. Walking down this concrete roadway was like passing through a weird technological jungle, where the giant trees were storage tanks, the creepers were pipelines that spread angularly from one to another of them, and the fungi were the bulbous valves that punctuated them at intervals.

He carried a flashlight in one hand and a truncheon in the other, which he had been given from the stock in the police cars. Having come from bed on his scooter direct to the scene of Ryan's injury, he had brought nothing but his notebook, which was always in the pocket either of his jacket or—in the summer—his shirt.

"And a notebook isn't much help right now," he muttered inside his helmet.

The clothing was stiflingly hot on this warm evening. It had no separate boots, only big floppy feet in one piece with the rest of the suit, so there was no way for air to get in except around the neck of the body section and through the ventilation slits crossing the front of the helmet. The flexible plastic window before his eyes was steaming up with the moisture his exertion generated. He flapped the bottom edges of the helmet back and forth to try and create a slight breeze for his perspiring face.

Suddenly a voice called from behind him, "Hey, I saw something!"

He whirled. One of the men without suits was pointing his flashlight down a dark alley between two buildings, whose doors identified them as spares and repair shops.

"Sellers!" Branksome said crisply. "You go first, will you? You can't come to much harm in that outfit!"

More than ever sorry that he had elected himself for this task, Sellers moved with the best grace he could to the mouth of the narrow, dark passageway. Peering along it, shining the beam of his torch, he caught a glimpse of movement.

"Yes, there's something there!" he exclaimed, and hurried forward.

Beyond the far end of the long huts, he found himself in what corresponded to a patch of undergrowth in the technological jungle he was crossing: a pattern of pipes running in every direction, marked with bands of red, white, yellow, and purple paint according to a code that identified the chemicals they contained. He almost tripped as he came on the first one, for here the light was less good than along the roadway.

"Over there!" he shouted, as he realized that a dark figure was making off on the far side of the pipes. Hampered by the clothing he wore, sweating a river, he set off in pursuit, leaping from pipe to pipe rather than trying to put his feet down between them.

"She's making for the wharf!" Branksome rapped from behind him. "Try and cut her off!"

Her? Without checking his progress from pipe to pipe, Sellers stared through the half-misted window of his helmet. Yes, of course, it was Miss Beeding—

"But it can't be her!" he said. "Unless I was right all along!"

He made a sudden spurt, and his foot caught in the tangle of pipes. He sprawled headlong, and the other two constables overtook him and raced ahead.

"You all right?" Branksome demanded, catching him up and helping him to his feet.

"Yes—yes, thanks, sarge. Just tripped over, that's all." Sellers scrambled to his feet. "But didn't you see who that was?"

"It *looks* like Miss Beeding," Branksome said after a moment of hesitation.

"It looks as much like her as the woman I saw at the Geddesley Mental Hospital," Sellers said bluntly.

They stared at each other for a few seconds. Then Branksome gestured him forward.

"Come on! We've got to get to the bottom of this!"

Directly beyond the tangle of pipes, they came in among the big storage tanks where the bulk chemicals were kept, each tank with an inspection ladder running up the side. Bright white placards with red letters were attached to the steel plates: DANGER! POISON! KEEP AWAY!

"Look, sarge, there she goes!" one of the other men in suits shouted, and raised his torch. Its beam showed the old woman's silhouette on one of the ladders leading up the side of a tank.

"Right, we've got her now!" Branksome said. "Surround the tank and—Christ, what does she think she's doing? Stop her! Hey! *Hey!*"

He dashed forward, but he was already too late. At the top of the ladder the figure dimly visible in the flashlight beam hesitated, glanced back, seemed to reach a decision, and dived into the liquid the tank contained.

There was a splash, another fainter, and—silence.

"Crude phenol," Sellers read from the identifying plaque on the side of the tank, and that was the last word any of them spoke until they had regained the gatekeeper's hut.

"Mr. Fleet's here!" Hedges announced eagerly. "Did you catch her?"

"No," Branksome snapped. "The bloody fool dived into a tank of phenol!"

Emerging from the hut in time to hear that, Fleet blanched. "Which one?" he demanded. "It'll contaminate the contents—I'll have to shut the valves off!"

"Is that all you can think of?" Branksome said sourly.

"Why not, sergeant?" another voice said from behind Fleet, and Leigh-Warden emerged from the gatekeeper's hut. "Don't we all care more about commercially profitable goods in this sick society of ours, than we do about mere human lives? Why, we make mass murder an industry every time we go to war—why should one old woman count especially?" He gave a grin.

"Shut up," Branksome said with uncharacteristic venom.

"In a moment," Leigh-Warden said. "Who was it? It's not too late yet for me to get a piece in the Stop Press of the London dailies, you know, and the evenings will willingly cover it in their noon editions."

There was a moment's silence. "We'll have to fish her body out in the morning and see," Branksome said at last.

"Really! So it wasn't Miss Beeding?" Leigh-Warden suggested.

"How could it have been?" Branksome countered.

"I don't know," Leigh-Warden said. "That's what I'm trying to find out." He smiled again, and moved toward his car.

XVIII

HAVING TAKEN HIS leave of everyone on board the *Jolly Roger,* Rory Dunstable came ashore with the supplies boat and went directly to the garage where he stored his car while he was at sea. Once he had checked it over and paid the fee for it, he drove slowly through the town to locate the photographic dealer to whom he had sent the film of his remarkable catch. The store had just opened for the day, and no one was there except the rather bored-looking elderly man behind the counter.

"You have a spool of Fujichrome for me," Rory said, and produced the receipt he had been given.

"Oh yes, *that* one," the proprietor nodded. "Been doing some experimental work, have you? Came out pretty well, by the look of it, except for the water on the lens, and that may have spoiled it—though it may be an effect you wanted, of course. Here you are!"

Rory blinked at him. With sudden decision, he opened the packet the man handed him and began to unreel the film.

"You don't want to do that, sir!" the proprietor exclaimed. "You'll get fingermarks on it—and you might scratch it!"

Rory ignored him, spilling foot after foot of the film on the counter as he scanned the images against the bright background of the shop window. He checked abruptly. Yes, there it was, emerging from the water the first time: a sleek fishlike body struggled to get free of the line. He unreeled some more. Now here was the second appearance—

And, exactly as the proprietor had said, there was water on the lens: spray thrown up by the creature's struggle, presumably. One large drop had landed on the side of the lens and distorted part of the image. But nonetheless . . .

He drew a deep breath. Yes, here on the film was evidence of something he hadn't trusted his own memory to confirm. The first time it showed above the water, this catch of his had been a fish. The second time, it had been . . .

"Something else," he murmured, and felt a chill go down his spine. This, definitely, had to be shown to experts, and at once. He began to rewind the film.

"How much do I owe you?" he said.

"Easy now," the man hanging on the ladder at the side of the phenol tank said, and moved the long grapple around in the dark, smelly liquid. "Ah!"

"Got something?" Fleet called from the ground below.

"Yes, I reckon this must be it," the man answered. "Just a mo' while I get a proper purchase on it!"

He removed one gauntlet to make sure the rope was moving freely over the pulley they had rigged at the side of the tank, then replaced it to make another stab with the grapple.

"Haul away!" he shouted, and the men on the rope below heaved in unison. In a little while they had tugged the object to the surface.

"Stop!" said the man at the top of the ladder, and peered down at what the grapple had raised for them.

"That's not an old woman," he said in a wondering tone. "That's a bloody fish! And I never heard of a fish being caught in a funnier place than this tank, b'God!"

He seized one of the creature's fins and heaved it over

the side of the tank by main force. Stepping back to avoid the drops of chemical it shed, Fleet said, "But that's not an old woman's body!"

"That's what there is in this tank," the man up the ladder said shortly, and began to descend the rungs.

"She *what*?" Sergeant Branksome said disbelievingly to the phone.

"She's vanished!" Dr. Nimms repeated in a frantic voice. "And one of my male nurses—young Stevens—has the same condition she had! He's standing where she was, in her cell, and he can hardly talk any better than she did!"

The door of the police station opened, and Sellers appeared, looking extremely tired. "Morning, sarge," he muttered. "I'm a bit late, aren't I? Sorry. I overslept after last night."

"Hey, come here!" Branksome snapped. "Excuse me, doctor—the constable I sent to see you just came in." He covered the mouthpiece. "Listen, Rodge, Miss Beeding seems to have escaped from Geddesley Mental Hospital."

"You mean it could have been her we saw last night at the chemical works?"

"No, that's what's so extraordinary! There wouldn't have been time for her to get from there to the plant—she was reported as being in her cell at midnight, when the night staff made their round of the wards. Just a moment." He uncovered the phone.

"Sorry to keep you waiting, doctor, but I want to get this perfectly straight. Now she was all right at midnight, yes? But this morning when you went to give her a relaxing injection so you could get her clothes off and everything she wasn't there ... ? Yes, I see. I fully understand. . . . No, I don't mean ... Could her condition have been contagious?"

Nimms blasted back his reply so loudly Sellers could hear it clearly. "There is no such thing as contagious amnesia! All I know is that this morning Stevens was found in her cell and there's no sign of her!"

"Well . . ." Branksome looked helpless. "I don't know what we can do, to be honest!" He seized a scratch pad. "We'll circulate a description of the missing woman, naturally, but it ought strictly to be Geddesley police who handle that. . . ." He listened. "Well, if you've already done that, doctor . . ."

Wincing, he set the phone down. "Why he should take it out on me, Lord knows!" he muttered.

The phone rang again. "You take it!" he rapped, and moved toward his office. Sellers hastened to obey.

"Brindown police station, Constable Sellers . . . Oh, Mr. Fleet! . . . *What?*" He made urgent signals to Branksome. "Are you sure? A fish? What kind of a fish?"

"Give me that!" Branksome snapped, and took the phone. "Mr. Fleet? Sergeant Branksome . . . Are you certain?"

There was a blur of noise from the other end. He said finally, "Well, sir, exactly how a fish could have . . . No, I appreciate that! But I was there, and I *saw* . . . Yes, sir, I do believe you! You drained the whole tank and there was nothing else! Well . . . Yes, please do that. It sounds as though an expert ought to look at this right away!"

He cradled the phone, sweating. "They put a grapple in the tank the old woman fell into, and they found a fish," he said. "They've drained the tank. There's no corpse in it. Rodge, was it a woman or not, that we saw climb that ladder and dive in?"

"It . . ." Sellers swallowed hard.

"Yes, I feel like that," Branksome said grimly. "He says he's going to load the fish on a pickup and get it over to the marine research station. I look forward to hearing what they have to say!" He hesitated.

"Do you know something?" he added. "I'm scared."

"So am I," Sellers acknowledged. "It's exactly as though the world has turned into a nightmare. Things aren't making sense any more!"

At the gate of the marine research station Rory Dunstable braked his car and got out. He went the rest of the way on foot, not wanting to risk the rough track. Soon he came upon a tall dark young man in a white coat who was carrying a large square Perspex container half-full of cloudy water in which things wiggled.

He called out, and the dark man turned to him with a sour expression.

"Yes, what is it?"

Taken aback by his rudeness, Rory said uncertainly, "Ah—I'm sorry to bother you, but I have a bit of film here that shows a fish I hooked the other day and didn't manage to land. I wondered if someone here could identify it for me."

"It's no part of our job to help people add detail to their fishing stories," the man said. "Good morning!"

And he strode away.

"The smug bastard!" Rory said under his breath. More than ever determined to go through with this, he walked on directly the man had vanished from sight. Shortly, he came to a small bungalow adjoining what he took to be the main building of the research station, with a mini-car parked outside it. As he passed, a pretty girl in white shorts and a green shirt appeared, carrying a scuba outfit, which she put in the car.

"Can I help you?" she called, noticing Rory.

He explained the reason for his visit, concluding, "So if

there is someone who could identify it for me, I'd be much obliged."

"I'll have a go, certainly," the girl said. He looked puzzled, and she added with a grin, "I'm Dr. Netta Reedwall—I work here. Don't worry!" as he started a confused apology. "Even my husband says he finds it hard to believe. Let's see the film. Oh, it's a movie film!"

"Yes, but you can see some detail even without a projector. I don't want to handle it too much, of course—"

"Well, locate the bit where it shows best," Netta suggested.

As Rory was complying, a man emerged from the house, dressed in an old check shirt and faded jeans, also carrying a scuba kit. Netta explained what she was doing and added, "My husband is the *other* Dr. Reedwall. Tom, this is—I'm sorry, I forgot to ask your name."

"Rory Dunstable. From Radio Jolly Roger. It was while I was fishing over the stern that I—ah! Here's the first time the thing appeared. Look."

He held the film very carefully so that Netta could look through it against the bright white background of the sunlit car roof. After a few moments' study of it, she began to frown.

"Tom, you take a look at it," she said, and moved aside. Tom did so, and almost at once his expression was as puzzled as hers.

"I'm afraid I can't place it," he admitted. "Still, the detail is difficult to make out, isn't it? Suppose we break out the projector for Mr. Dunstable, darling? It would only take a few minutes."

"That's very kind of you," Rory said. "But I haven't finished showing you the oddest thing about this fish." He reeled along the strip of film.

"Now look at it," he muttered, and waited tensely while

they inspected the frame in which the fish made its second visit to the air.

Tom whistled between his teeth. "That's a squid," he said positively.

"Yes, but since when did squids have tails?" Rory countered. "Where—? Ah, yes! This next frame shows it best. See?"

Both Tom and Netta were staring in astonishment when the noise of an engine was heard. They glanced up to see a small pickup truck bouncing down the track toward them. It halted at the first building and turned into a parking space. As it came broadside to them they could see that something under a tarpaulin lay on the load platform.

A man jumped out and hurried toward them.

"Why, it's Mr. Fleet from the chemical works, isn't it?" Netta exclaimed.

"Morning!" Fleet called. "Thank goodness you're here —I suddenly realized it was Saturday and I didn't think of phoning before I left the plant. I was too excited. Come and see this, will you?"

He spun on his heel. With a muttered apology, Tom and Netta followed him, leaving Rory to roll up his film again.

Fleet peeled back the tarpaulin, and revealed the bulky object underneath as a fish, stinking of phenol and badly discolored by immersion in the chemical.

"What is it?" he rapped.

"It looks like a *Hippoglossus*," Tom said after a pause. "A halibut, that is. Netta?"

"Well . . . Yes, I suppose so," Netta agreed after a few seconds of thought. "Only there's something wrong with it. It's deformed, or diseased, or something. I can't quite spot what's wrong, but—"

She stared at the big fish's gaping mouth, then cautiously prodded at the gill slits behind the head.

Meantime, Rory had rewound his film on its spool and come curiously over to join them. Whoever had landed this, he thought, had every right to be pleased; it must weigh a hundred pounds or more. Appraising it with an angler's eye, he walked to the rear of the truck, and suddenly gasped.

"The tail!" he said.

Fleet stared at him. "What's wrong with its tail?" he snapped.

"Well, I'm no expert—I just have a lay interest in fishing, but . . ." Rory appealed to Netta with his eyes.

"That's right!" she said. "Tom, see?"

"Of course!" her husband exclaimed. He bent over the platform and prodded at the organ in question.

"Will someone tell me what *about* the tail?" Fleet burst out.

"Uh—" Rory stepped into the breach. "Well, a fish's rear fins are set vertically to the body. This creature's tail is horizontal, like the flukes of a sea-going mammal—a whale, or a dolphin." He hesitated. "Wasn't that why you brought it here—because it's a mutation of some kind you want to have identified?"

"No," Fleet said. "I brought it here because . . . Dr. Reedwall, you know about the crazy old woman who attacked the Irishman on the beach last night?"

"Yes." Tom raised a puzzled face. "What's she got to do with this thing?"

"We cornered her—at least the police did—in our works. And she was driven up a ladder when they surrounded her, and when she got to the top she dived into a storage tank full of phenol. And this morning, when we drained the tank, all we could find in it was—*this*!"

XIX

"WHAT ON EARTH is going on?" Dr. Innis said in a vexed tone to Sam Fletcher.

Fletcher glanced up. They were in Innis's office going over the latest reports from the experimental shellfish sites. He was not in a good temper—he never was on the one Saturday morning in four when he was on duty. That this was supposed to be a free weekend for Dr. Innis was a point he could not have cared less about.

"Oh, some angler wanted us to identify a fish he'd lost. He brought a film along. *I* told him to get out."

Dr. Innis rose and peered out of the window. "That fish hasn't been lost," he said. "And it's a sizable specimen, too. A *Hippoglossus*, I think. Let's go and take a look."

Sighing, Fletcher accompanied him out to the pickup. Tom hailed Dr. Innis as soon as they appeared.

"Dr. Innis! Have you ever seen anything like this?"

He rapidly explained the circumstances that had led to the fish being brought here, and pointed out other things besides the tail that were unusual. The body was the wrong shape behind the gills—too cylindrical. The scales were of a curious unfishlike type, arranged in a sort of honeycomb pattern, and there were loose folds of skin hanging all around the midriff section.

"Bless my soul, this is extraordinary!" Dr. Innis said, and produced a pocket glass to inspect the scales more closely.

Fletcher gave a loud sigh. "Dr. Innis, are we through for the morning, then?"

Innis raised his head. "What?"

"If we aren't going to finish what we were doing, I'd like to quit. It is Saturday, after all!"

"My dear fellow, this is clearly a sport of some kind, and a most remarkable catch!"

"You believe this farrago of nonsense about it being found in a tank of chemicals?" Fletcher said with a curl of his lip. "It's a hoax, obviously, and not a very clever one!"

For a moment his eyes and Dr. Innis's locked. Then the older man said, "Leave by all means. I would rather not have you around to accuse me of failing to see through a hoax."

Fletcher's dark, handsome face colored briefly. Then, with a forced expression of contempt, he spun on his heel.

As though nothing had happened, Dr. Innis said, "Dr. Reedwall, what do you make of this?"

Tom hesitated. He said at length, "Well, if one could do with fish as unscrupulous dealers do with cars—weld the back half of one on the front of another—I'd say that would account for it."

"I can think of another explanation, which is equally ridiculous," Netta offered.

"Let's hear it, young lady," Innis said. "This object is patently ridiculous anyway, but I have no reason to doubt the veracity of our friend Mr. Fleet, have I? As the celebrated Sherlock Holmes was accustomed to remark, when you have eliminated the impossible, what remains, however improbable, must be the truth."

Standing a little aside, Rory decided that he rather liked this pugnacious elderly scientist.

"I'd never have thought of this," Netta said apologetically, "but for the film Mr. Dunstable brought with him.

It seems to me that—well, this *thing*, whatever it is, might be in a process of change from one form to another. . . ."

She let her voice trail away uncertainly.

"From one form to another?" Dr. Innis echoed. "My dear young woman, creatures of this size don't undergo metamorphosis!"

"Please show him your film, Mr. Dunstable," Netta said.

Rory, complying, waited while Dr. Innis examined the pictures, looking baffled. He said finally, "I—ah—I have no reason to doubt your veracity either, sir. But at the moment I'm wondering if I have reason to doubt my sanity!"

"Let's get this thing into the lab," Tom proposed. "If we find it's as peculiar inside as it seems to be outside, we'll have something definite to go on!"

"Do you mind if I come along?" Rory ventured. "Fishing is only a hobby of mine, but I am kind of interested."

"By all means," Innis said. "Though you know we're trying to render anglers like you obsolete, don't you? The next generation will have to be farmers of the sea, not hunters! All right, this way—come along!"

"Lord knows how Miss Beeding managed to get away from the hospital," Branksome sighed, moving toward the door. "But if she managed it she might well head for home, mightn't she? I think I'll run over and check the Warrinder farm. Can you hold the fort for an hour?"

"Of course, sarge," Sellers said. "But—didn't I gather that she overpowered one of the male nurses? Might it not be dangerous to go on your own?"

"I'm going to be bloody careful, believe me!" Branksome said. "I told you—I'm frightened. I can't figure out what's going on around here!" He drew a deep breath.

"We know Miss Beeding couldn't punch her way out of

a wet paper bag, don't we? Yet here, within a few hours, we get reports of some old woman answering her description who costs that big burly Irish workman his right hand, *and* of her getting the better of a trained male nurse in a mental hospital! What's worse, there's this crazy story from the chemical works. It's as though there were *two* Miss Beedings, neither of them the same as the one we know."

"That's what Doreen said," Sellers muttered. "But like she went on to say, there's bound to be some perfectly rational explanation, isn't there?"

"Don't be too confident," Branksome said grayly. "When you get a bit older, Rodge, you'll realize there are some things you can never get to the bottom of. See you later."

It took him only a short time to reach the vicinity of the Warrinder farm. A quick tour of the surrounding fields, a check of the ruined house, and he was sure Miss Beeding was nowhere nearby.

However, he felt reluctant to go back to the station at once and carry on with the boring daily routine of his job. He walked at random westward from the ruined farm, and before he realized he had come so far he found he was at the marine research station. Parked near one of the buildings on the inland side, he saw a pickup labeled "Organic Acids Ltd."

Of course. The fish Fleet said they found in the tank where a woman's body should have been!

Suddenly desperate to know if these experts had managed to reach the rational explanation Sellers had been talking about, he hurried into the research station precincts, looking about him for signs of life. Belatedly, he realized it was Saturday; Fleet might not have found anyone here but a duty technician.

He was about to turn dispiritedly and walk back to

where he had left his car when the door of one of the buildings opened and a party of people emerged, talking loudly: Dr. Innis, the Reedwalls, Fleet, and a man he didn't recognize.

Spotting him, Tom Reedwall broke off what he was saying and called out.

"Sergeant! Come here! How lucky you turned up—you're exactly the sort of person we need!"

And he added to his companions, "Look, the sergeant's been trained in sifting evidence, presumably. Shall we put it to him and see what he makes of it?"

After a moment the others nodded. But even as he waited to find out why they wanted him to referee their argument, Branksome wondered at the expressions they all wore.

They looked *terrified*.

XX

BROOKING NO DENIAL, Tom hurried the others, including Branksome, toward a door which bore the legend MAIN LABORATORY. Opening it, he revealed a room whose walls were lined with benches bearing jars of reagent, cans of nutrient additives, samples of fish spawn and young spat in Perspex containers like the one Fletcher had been carrying when Rory had met him, and several microscopes.

On a large plastic-topped table in the center of the floor lay the carcass of the fish which Fleet had brought in. Belly uppermost, it had been dissected with skill and precision. Some of its internal organs had been removed and placed in sample jars, exposing the skeletal structure.

"Do you know anything about the anatomy of fish?" Tom demanded of Branksome. The sergeant hesitated.

"Well, I suppose I studied it during biology lessons at school, but that was a long time ago."

"But you possibly remember the difference between the tails of fish and aquatic mammals?"

"Ah—yes, I think so. Fish have fins and whales have flukes, isn't that right?"

"Full marks. Well, look at the tail on this thing! The front end's a fish, all right, but the rear end isn't—see?" And, as Branksome gave an awed nod, Tom continued: "But the internal organization is equally funny. See this group of bones here? That's a bloody pelvis, with two rudimentary legs extending into the flukes! And what's more, the halibut is a teleost, but watch!"

Seizing one of the scalpels used for the dissection, he thrust it into one of the exposed bones. It sank an inch deep.

"Soft—cartilaginous!" he exclaimed. "But the teleosts are hard-boned fishes; their skeleton ought to be nearly as hard as yours or mine."

"I'm not quite sure I follow that," Branksome said.

"Some fish do have cartilaginous bones," Netta supplied. "What we call the elasmobranchs—like sharks, for instance. A halibut, which is what this would be if the head and gills were a fair sample of the rest, ought to have a bony skeleton."

"I get you," Branksome nodded. "But . . ." He swallowed hard. "But wasn't this what was found when you drained your tank, Mr. Fleet?"

Fleet looked extremely unhappy. He said, "Please don't ask me to explain what's happened, Sergeant. Unless someone managed to haul the woman's body out during the night, and replace it with this, I don't understand how a fish could *be* in our tank!"

"You kept an overnight watch on the tank, did you?"

"Yes, I gave our Mr. Hedges special instructions. And he's most reliable. After all, he did spot the old woman last night, didn't he?"

"In any case," Netta said, "what reason could anyone have for undertaking such a dangerous job as swapping this improbable fish for a dead woman?"

"But in that case—" Branksome stopped dead.

"Go on, sergeant," sighed Dr. Innis. "I don't think I shall like what you're about to say, but I feel I shall be compelled to agree with it."

"I was going to say if there wasn't a chance of substitution," Branksome muttered, "then this must be the thing we—we mistook for a woman diving into the tank."

The others exchanged worried glances. "I'm afraid that

does seem right," Tom said. "And if it hadn't been for Mr. Dunstable coming here this morning I'd have dismissed it out of hand. But—well, come along to my office. We set up the projector to view his film, and we'd just seen it twice over when you turned up. It's alarming, to put it mildly!"

In a small office, where piles of documents stacked on shelves jostled volumes of scientific journals with titles like *The Oceanographer* and *Marine Biology Abstracts*, Rory took efficient charge of the projector. Having drawn the curtains, Tom sat down along with the others in some chairs that were assembled haphazardly, facing the screen on his desk. The range was too short to give a large picture, but the detail was sharp and the lighting good.

First they saw an expanse of sea viewed over the stern of a ship. Heads and arms crossed the field of view; they caught a glimpse of Rory, with another more heavily built young man, hauling on his fishing line. Then something began to show at the surface. A blur of spray surrounded it, but Rory deftly stopped the projector at a frame which showed that it was indeed a fish. Having let that point sink in, he restarted the motor and ran it until the second time the creature visited the air. Now, in spite of the drop of spray that had landed on the lens and spoiled the detail, it was incontestable that the shape of the catch had changed.

They all looked expectantly at Branksome. He said feebly, "This film—has it been doctored?"

"I can get you half a dozen witnesses to say it shows precisely what happened!" Rory snapped.

"I give up," Branksome said. "Dr. Innis, what am I supposed to make of it?"

"Excuse me," Netta put in. "I think there's one more point we need to cover. I just thought of it. Let's go back to the lab."

With much shuffling of chairs, they did so. Going into the lab ahead of the others, Netta seized a glass rod from one of the benches and used it as a pointer to tease up one of the flaps of loose skin around the creature's middle section which they had already brought to Branksome's attention.

"Sergeant, imagine this fish stood upright, like a human being. What would this loose skin remind you of?"

"A—a skirt, I suppose," Branksome ventured, and all the others gave satisfied nods.

"It's contrary to everything I ever heard of before," Dr. Innis sighed, "but for want of a more reasonable explanation I must accept that a case has been established. You formulated the original hypothesis, young lady—let's hear you spell it out in detail."

"That there is a creature capable of changing its form," Netta shrugged. She was very pale. "Or perhaps it wouldn't be *a* creature—I put a few scrapings from this thing under the microscope and although I haven't had time to examine them very closely there's a vast difference not only between this and ordinary piscine cellular material but also from one specimen to the next. It might perhaps be a colony-creature, like a jellyfish or a nautilus."

"But where could a creature like that derive its genetic material from?" Tom demanded. "You'd expect it to be almost fluid, if it were capable of such radical changes of shape!"

"The facts stand, though," Netta countered. "I say that this thing must be the same as what Sergeant Branksome and Paddy Ryan and everyone else mistook for an old woman. I could imagine it—oh—deriving the necessary DNA and RNA codes from its prey instead of from its own inheritance, merely modifying the prey's gene code in order to preserve the identity of the species. It must clearly reproduce asexually—most likely, by simple fission."

"Lord!" Tom said, staring into nowhere. "It does fit, doesn't it?"

"Too well," Dr. Innis muttered. "For my liking, at least. Go on, young lady!"

Very conscious of them staring at her, especially the laymen—Rory, Branksome, and Fleet—Netta said, "Well ... All right. We have to assume two forms of change which the creature is capable of. First, simple camouflage. After all, a predator could hardly have a better assurance of access to its food supply than the power to disguise itself as one of them. And this talent would carry a built-in advantage if the prey ran short. As soon as the creature met a member of some other edible species, it would change form to match a shoal of that one instead of the former.

"And the second type of change is exemplified by Rory's film, isn't it? In danger of its life, what he caught did appear to try a shift from the fishlike to the squidlike form. Perhaps there's a rudimentary cellular memory that can override the coding of the ingested gene material from the last feed."

"I think I follow this," Tom said, frowning. "Now this appears to be a fairly massive creature, judging by the specimen we have here. Would it not be reasonable to suppose that the larger the creature became after countless divisions, each time ingesting a slightly bigger prey, the more difficult it would find the change, and the more likely it would be to run short of likely quarry? There aren't many hundred-pound fish in these waters."

"Perhaps this has strayed here from the deep ocean," Netta agreed. "But there's something else which fits my guess: the way the—the so-called old woman dived into

Mr. Fleet's phenol tank. In a panic, the creature probably mistook it for water, its natural refuge."

"And is that where Paddy Ryan's hand went?" Tom said suddenly.

"I think it must be," Netta said dispiritedly. "The creature must have been due to divide again, and before doing so it wanted to feed to provide adequate protoplasm for the daughter-creature. The organs of this animal *must* be as unspecialized as the rest of it. To engulf its prey it must envelóp it, rather than eat it. And for that you'd need a fierce digestive fluid secreted by the integument."

"But presumably the ingested protoplasm must exceed a certain critical value," Dr. Innis said. "Otherwise there will be a conflict of cellular memories, and—"

"And you'd wind up with some hybrid form like this," Tom supplied, indicating the thing on the dissecting table.

For a moment there was silence. Suddenly Rory said, "If I've followed this, you're saying that it needs a—a model, right? And its food serves as one. But big fish are hard to find here. Instead of a fish, this time it took a *human* body. Christ, what an awful thought!" He shuddered. "But in that case— Sergeant, what's wrong?"

They all turned to Branksome.

"I know where it could have got one!" he exclaimed. "The pilot of that plane which crashed last Monday!"

"Lord, yes!" Innis said. "That fits, too. And if it acquired some kind of conscious memory along with the cellular memory guiding its change of shape, then it would have felt the impulse to work its way ashore."

"And I know when it came ashore, and where," Branksome said. "And after it came ashore, it found Miss Beeding, and—and took her over, and . . . Where's the nearest phone?"

He jumped to his feet.

"In my office," Tom said. "What's the hurry?"

"Don't you realize there's one of these things up at Geddesley Mental Hospital?" Branksome rapped, and dashed for the door. On the threshold, he checked and turned back.

"Wait a moment. Every time it feeds it takes on a new form, that right?"

"Presumably," Tom agreed.

"And the new form is—is twins?"

"Well, that would explain everything very neatly, wouldn't it?"

"Then where in hell can the other Stevens be?"

They looked at him blankly. He passed a tired hand over his face. "Sorry, you wouldn't have heard about that. The 'Miss Beeding' in the hospital behaved in all sorts of odd ways—seemed to have forgotten half the words of the language, according to Dr. Nimms, turned violent and wouldn't let anyone touch her . . ."

"To stop someone finding out that her 'clothes' were only a specialized form of skin!" Tom rapped.

"Possibly. Anyway, during the night she overpowered a male nurse called Stevens, and now there must be *two* of him, right? But only one was reported from the hospital. The other one must have got away!"

"You say she remembered only half the words in the language?" Dr. Innis whispered, face drawn.

"That's right."

"But the fact that the creature remembered any of them at all is incredible—and terrifying!" Innis jumped to his feet. "If it absorbed the power of speech and rational thought along with the shape of the human body, then after a few more feeds the creatures are going to be fully equipped with everything they need—language, comprehension, everything—to pass themselves off as members of our own species!"

There was a frozen pause. At last Branksome stirred.

He said, "Well, however that may be, there's one thing I must do right away—tell Dr. Nimms that what he's got in Miss Beeding's cell isn't a man, but a bloody fish!"

XXI

ALERTED BY THE phone call, looking harassed, Dr. Nimms greeted Sergeant Branksome and the bewildered Chief Inspector Neville—whom only the scientific reputation of Dr. Innis had persuaded to come out from county police headquarters—as soon as they arrived at the mental hospital.

"I couldn't make head or tail of this story you spun me over the phone," he declared to the sergeant. "But directly you'd spoken to me I went back to take another look at—at Stevens, or whoever it is. We're dreadfully busy here, understaffed and overworked, and frankly all I'd done up until then was to establish that his condition matched Miss Beeding's in every particular. Which it did seem to—words missing from what he said, sudden irrational violence if I tried to touch him. But since your call I've been back to take a fresh look, and frankly I can't account for what I found, unless I accept this incredible hypothesis you described to me." As he talked, he was hurrying them down corridors and across wards; the staff they met had expressions as worried and depressed as the patients.

"Here we are," he said finally, halting before the door of a security cell with a peephole in it. "The things I've noticed now that I overlooked before are fantastic. Stevens is—was—I don't know which I ought to say! Was a burly young man, anyway. Muscular. Rather heavy-set. Well, whoever or whatever is standing in there is a good two or

147

three inches shorter than he ought to be. I checked by measuring the height of the window in the next cell; they're identical. Not so brawny, either. Puffy and flabby, like Miss Beeding. And his clothes, too. They're wrong. They look as slick and shiny—sort of *wet*—as though they were made out of PVC. See for yourself."

He slid back the hatch in the door and gestured for Branksome and Neville to peer through.

"You're certain about what you've just told us?" Neville said finally.

"About his height and build? Yes, absolutely positive," Nimms declared.

"In that case, for want of a better explanation, I suppose we'll have to act on what Dr. Innis says," Neville sighed. "Though heaven knows how I'm going to convince the Chief Constable." He brightened a little. "Oh, no! The old so-and-so is away this weekend; I only have the ACC to deal with, and that's a different proposition." -

Turning away and closing the hatch as though to escape the baleful, fixed glare of the pseudohuman creature within, he went on, "If I've understood correctly, the main problem is that there's some sort of identical twin of your male nurse wandering around—that right, sergeant?"

Branksome nodded.

"How did he get out of the hospital? Why wasn't his absence noticed earlier?"

Nimms looked abject. He said, "There was an error—a hundred-to-one chance—in the staffing roster. The person who compiled it put down the weekday staffing times instead of the weekend ones, and we have a new duty nurse on this morning, who didn't realize he was coming in an hour later than he should have. When he found out, he naturally assumed Stevens had handed over to the duty female nurse—who'd come in at the right time—and it wasn't till I arrived myself that the situation came clear."

"So he could have walked out—I mean *it* could have walked out—unchallenged by your gatekeeper, or anyone?" Neville said.

"Precisely."

"So he's had—how long to get away?"

Nimms glanced at his watch. "Oh, four good hours, maybe longer."

"Could this creature make out among the general public well enough to conceal its true identity?" Neville demanded.

"I—I don't know. I suppose it probably could," Nimms muttered. "After all, according to what I've been told by your sergeant on the phone, it won't need to eat except in its own disgusting fashion, and that not for some time yet, so it won't be caught through not knowing how to pay for things, or anything else obvious. And come to think of it: if it acquired Miss Beeding's memory, or rather divided the memory in half, that accounts neatly for her apparent partial amnesia. Common words, repeated thousands of times a day, like 'and' or 'the,' she had a perfect command of. Only the rarer words seemed to escape her, and though some of them were what you might think of as common in fact, now I look back on it they might possibly have been words that she herself seldom employed. Not that I knew her before she came here, of course." He was almost gabbling, as though to distract himself from the new terrifying concepts they were all struggling to adapt their minds to.

"But now she'll have acquired a second half-set of memories, won't she?" Branksome said quietly. Nimms gave a miserable nod.

"Assuming this hypothesis is the true one," he confirmed.

"In that case, even if there's only a shred of truth in it, we've got to act fast," Neville said with decision. "In fact, before this—this creature impersonating Stevens becomes ready to feed again. How long have we got?"

Branksome hesitated, frowning as he made some mental calculations. "If it's true that the creature was seen coming out of the sea by this pop group I told you about, sir," he said, "the period between—uh—feeds and divisions must be of the order of two days. But you'd better check that with the experts at the marine research station."

"I certainly will," Neville promised. "And the first thing we'd better do, difficult or not, must be to have them examine the pseudo-Stevens in that cell!"

"But the night watchman at the chemical plant had his sleeve burned through when the thing touched him," Branksome objected. "And that poor devil of an Irishman—"

"I don't think there's any need to worry about that for a few hours at least," Nevile cut in. "Doctor, did any of your staff suffer acid burns in trying to handle Miss Beeding—as you thought she was?"

Nimms held up his own right hand, palm out. "I took a grip on her myself," he said. "The only reason I had to let go was because she was too strong for me."

"Good. Presumably, sergeant," Neville added to Branksome, "the acid—whatever it is—is only secreted when the creature wants to feed. We have time to put this one in a safer place. Perhaps there's a suitable cage at the marine research station. Go find a phone and ask the director, will you? Until we can get some top-level experts down from London—and on Saturday that's likely to be difficult—we're going to have to rely on Dr. Innis and his staff for advice."

And, as Branksome hurried away to comply, he turned to Nimms with a wry expression.

"I can tell what you're thinking, Doctor," he said.

"That I'm accepting a fantastic story much too quickly, and taking it too seriously. Correct?"

Nimms shook his head. He said in a strained voice, "Not at all. It's never entered my head before to conceive of a creature that could not just imitate the form of another animal—after all, there are stick insects, aren't there, and fish that have fins that resemble seaweed, and so on?—but could also steal the memory of what they were copying. But thinking back over the way Miss Beeding behaved, I find more and more that this would explain her actions down to the last jot."

He mopped his face with a large white handkerchief.

"I'm even beginning to wonder," he concluded, "whether creatures like this have turned up before and been mistaken for simple lunatics because there wasn't any alternative explanation!"

"I doubt it," Neville said. "This creature causes someone to disappear each time it feeds, as I understand it. That would have—ah—attracted attention, to put it mildly. But," he concluded in a changed tone, "whether or not such things have cropped up before, we seem to have got one now and I'd better start doing something about it!"

"That was Sam Fletcher's landlady," Tom said, cradling the phone. "He's not there and she doesn't expect him back before Monday morning. And she doesn't know where he's gone."

"Too bad," Netta said cynically, drawing down from the shelves of the office a stack of reference books on piscine anatomy and cell structure. "I'm happier without him, let's face it."

"Bastard or not, he's good at his job," Tom countered with a worried frown. "And unless we can raise someone from the Natural History Museum or the Oceanographical Institute we're going to be thrown completely on local resources until Monday. And this is a bigger problem than I ever expected to tackle when I picked marine biology as a career."

"There aren't half a dozen men in the country better than Doc Innis, and you know it," Netta said. "One of him is worth two Sam Fletchers any day of the week. Come on, give me a hand with this lot."

Tom was about to relieve her of some of the heavy volumes when the phone rang. He picked it up and answered, "Marine Research Station, Brindown ... Who is that? ... Just a moment, I'll fetch him for you."

Dropping the receiver on the table, he darted for the door. "Sergeant Branksome, calling from Geddesley Mental Hospital," he explained. "Wants to speak to the doc, urgently."

A minute later he returned with Innis, who was wiping from his hands a foul, smelly mixture of fish blood and phenol. He picked up the phone between finger and thumb, and spoke.

"Innis here, sergeant—what is it? ... But for goodness' sake, sergeant! ... Yes, I appreciate that. ... Nonetheless, we simply aren't equipped to handle ..."

Tom and Netta exchanged worried glances.

"All right, all right," Innis conceded finally. "But for goodness' sake make sure it's properly under control! We've barely started to study the specimen that was found at the chemical works, and that's badly affected by the phenol it was immersed in all night. It may be very strong, it may be able to secrete that acid that took off the workman's hand. ... Oh, very probably, but if it can change shape voluntarily, as it appeared to from that film of Mr. Dunstable's ... Very well, very well! It is probably better off here than in a police station or a hospital, and we are isolated, as you say. I give up!"

He put the phone down and looked at his companions.

"The chief inspector has apparently decided that the—ah—specimen at the mental hospital ought to be taken somewhere else, and he's chosen this place. We can put it in the constant-temperature room, I suppose. That would be big enough, wouldn't it?"

"And what are we supposed to do with it when it arrives?" Tom demanded.

"Study it," Innis said with a helpless shrug. "They have the mistaken impression that we're the—ah—available experts. Unless I'm greatly in error myself, though, this is something regarding which experts do not yet exist."

He briskened. "Still, the prospect of becoming one is a challenge, at least! Shall we go and inspect the constant-temperature room and see if it's really suitable?"

"But this is ridiculous!" Netta said. "Surely the thing is already securely locked up in a cell at the hospital, and I suppose it has barred windows and so on—why move it at all? Isn't the real danger from the one which is at large impersonating the male nurse?"

"When you've become as prematurely old as I have," Innis sighed, "and when you've had more experience arguing with government administrators, you'll realize how futile it is to try and handle the—ah—the *official mind* on a rational basis. We shall simply have to make the best of it, I'm afraid."

XXII

"Is THIS WHERE you propose to put the creature?" said Chief Inspector Neville.

Innis shrugged. "This incubation house is the most solidly built part of the station, and this is the most secure room in it. It can be cleared fairly easily. And the only alternative would be a timber shed."

Neville looked around, frowning a little. They stood in a windowless room about eight feet by fifteen, lit by a single overhead fluorescent. The walls were of concrete, lined with shelves from near floor-level to as high as a man could reach, and the door was of metal sheets on a wooden frame with a layer of insulating material between the plates, and could, as he saw, be locked.

"What do you use this room for?" he asked.

"It's a constant-temperature room," Innis explained. "The design prevents the temperature from varying more than two or three degrees regardless of the season. This enables us to control the growing conditions of fish and spawn very closely."

"That's why it hasn't any windows?"

"Of course."

"But the air's fresh—is there a ventilator?"

Innis dropped to one knee and pointed to a mesh grille under the lowest set of shelves. "This runs directly to the edge of the sea, so the air is always humid, and there's a thermostatically controlled conditioner partway along the pipe."

"I think it'll do very well," Neville said at length. "If that grille is secure . . ." He linked three fingers in the mesh and gave a tug; the frame held. "Anyway, nothing as large as a man could get down that pipe, by the look of it." He straightened, dusting his hands together. "Fine, I'll have it brought here right away."

"There are some other problems, you know," Innis objected. "For example, the corridor here leads to several rooms besides this one." He stepped halfway through the doorway and pointed. "We can't use it as—what would you call it?—a lock, I suppose you'd say. And we'll presumably have to get in and out of the constant-temperature room to examine the thing, otherwise why have it here?"

"I see what you mean," Neville frowned. "Yes, if it turns fractious and starts to secrete its acid again . . . Ah, I have an idea. I believe they have protective clothing at the Organic Acids plant. I'll have a set loaned to you. That ought to enable whoever's in charge to—well—to handle it, if necessary."

"This thing only looks human," Innis said. "It may be inhumanly strong. It may be impervious to the sort of injury a human being is incapacitated by. Above all it may not feel pain. And one of my staff is a fragile young lady. I'm not particularly happy, chief inspector!"

"I'll make certain you have a roster of husky young constables to assist you over the weekend," Neville promised. "And on Monday morning presumably you'll not only have your full staff here—you'll have whoever you can reach to help you study the creature, right?"

"I've left half a dozen messages with top authorities on marine biology, asking them to get here as fast as possible. But some of them are elderly men themselves. No, I'm afraid I must ask for a permanent guard until the creature is removed to a really safe place. And I'll take the protective suiting with pleasure, preferably before the creature gets here."

"I'll do my best," Neville sighed. "But you do realize, don't you, that there's another creature on the loose as well as the one safely locked up in Geddesley Mental Hospital? I have to catch that beast before it does any more harm!"

"Tom, quick—look at this!" Netta exclaimed, slipping off the stool on which she had perched to stare down the barrel of the three-thousand-power microscope.

Catching the note of urgency in her voice, Tom hastily deposited the latest tissue sample he was preparing with the thermal microtome on its slide and answered her call. The lab's windows were open to let out the horrible stench of fish blood and phenol, and some flies had come buzzing in to investigate, but they didn't like the unwholesome tang of the exposed flesh on the dissecting table and were flitting around in frustration.

He made a hasty adjustment of the focus and whistled under his breath. He had prepared this sample only a few moments ago. What he ought to have seen was a conventional tissue-thin segment of the creature's integument, the cells arranged in an irregular network with their nuclei and external walls clearly defined. Instead, he was watching a writhing blob of featureless protoplasm, in which dark smears coagulated and almost at once dissipated again.

"Well?" Netta demanded.

"Still alive, at least on the cellular level, after a night's immersion in the phenol tank!" Tom grunted. "This is a very tough animal, isn't it?"

"Yes, but worse than that—maybe you were too late to catch the final breakdown of the cell walls, but I saw it." Netta pushed back her fair hair dispiritedly. "This thing must presumably carry its species-memory somewhere, mustn't it? Otherwise whatever it took over would simply become it, and would feed and reproduce from then on in conventional fashion—correct?"

Tom nodded. "I see what you mean. Even the chromosomes look as though they're breaking up in this miniature stew you have here." He added after a moment's thought: "Of course, this could be the death process, couldn't it?" He didn't sound very reassuring.

"Can't be that," Netta said positively. She fished out a cigarette and lit it, her pretty face drawn into a frown. "I've been working it out. This creature must have to dissolve and almost instantly reform everything, including the bones of its prey. Otherwise some much bigger creature might come along and gobble it up while it was still formless and defenseless, and being swilled around in the digestive tract of a whale or a big squid would probably be too much even for something which is, as you say, very tough."

"Maybe the acid it secretes itself protects it," Tom countered. "The stuff that took off Paddy's hand must foul the water for some distance around and other bigger fish would probably not care for the taste."

"That's a point, but obviously it must have to avoid secreting any more of the acid than it can help," Netta argued. "If it's going to reconstruct itself in the new form, it'll need to stop the acid being generated as soon as it can—otherwise it would simply digest the new cells as fast as they formed, right?"

"Yes, I suppose so. Also, it wouldn't want to waste any more of its available substance that it could help, and the acid must get diluted and carried off in the sea, hm?"

"Precisely." Netta stared at the microscope and failed to repress a shudder. "So it must have—well, I imagine you'd call them 'filterable chromosomes,' like filterable viruses—capable of making their way through the cell walls of the prey and taking them over rather than making them over. The whole process must be very fast indeed. Even when the creature becomes as massive as a man, I don't see how it could take longer than—well—let's say an hour at the outside. And it may only be a few minutes, for all we can tell at present."

She broke off suddenly. "I say, I suppose this one on the table is safe to be left around, is it? I never expected to see the cells dissociating under the microscope the way they're doing—I thought they'd be permanently inactivated."

"That's a point," Tom agreed. "But I think you've hit on the last flicker of life. I mean, I've been over that thing from nose to tail while I was preparing the slides, and I haven't seen a sign of movement on the macro level."

Netta relaxed very slightly. But she still looked very worried as she said, "I wish we had a decent electron microscope here! I'd like to get right down to the level where this beast keeps its true nature. . . . Tom, where do you think it could have come from?"

"Goodness knows."

"Do you think it's a recent mutation, or just something we've never run across before, like the coelacanth?"

"I've been wondering about that," Tom muttered. "And I'm very much afraid it probably is recent. On the face of it, this must be one of the most successful life forms ever evolved, and if it had been around for even a million years I'd have expected it to take over the entire ocean!"

"What could have caused it?"

"You're asking me?" Tom sighed. "But I can guess, and so can you. In the past couple of decades we've put more mutation-inducing substances into the sea than you'd normally expect in several centuries—fallout from H-bomb tests, canned waste from nuclear power stations . . ."

Outside, there were footsteps and the sound of Inkos

umping to his feet, tail going thump-thump against the
wall of the lab. He was never allowed into any of the labs
or offices, but hated to be further away from his master
and mistress than the door of the room where they were.
Dr. Innis opened the door and peered in.

"Ah, you're by yourselves!" he exclaimed.

"Yes, Mr. Fleet had to get home, and I think Mr.
Dunstable had to go back to London for an appointment,"
Tom said.

Behind Innis, Neville scowled. "Damnation! I particu-
arly wanted to have a word with them. I'm sure I can rely
on your discretion, but I'm very much afraid of what
might happen if a garbled version of this affair got out to
he press." He hesitated. "Matter of fact," he concluded,
"for all I know it may already be too late to stop it. I
heard from Sergeant Branksome that a local reporter had
been taking a great interest in the mystery."

"Oh, you must mean Leigh-Warden," Tom said, and
added to Netta when she looked puzzled, "Sam Fletcher's
chum, that he goes drinking with occasionally."

He went on, "But I don't think you need worry, Chief
Inspector. Mr. Fleet was in a positive lather of anxiety
about the bad publicity his firm would get if it were
known someone—or *something*—had drowned in a tank
of supposedly pure chemical, and as for Mr. Dunstable,
he struck me as pretty level-headed and not likely to rush
off to the papers."

"I'm glad to have your opinion," Neville said with a
shrug. "Nonetheless, he's in a publicity-hungry business,
isn't he? I hadn't realized who he was until Dr. Innis
mentioned it just a moment ago." Briskening, he straightened.

"Well, I'll go and arrange your—ah—special delivery!"

"Mr. Neville—just a moment!" Netta stepped forward.
Tom and I were just talking about this creature, and if

159

we're right in the way we've worked out its metabolism, a live specimen is going to be extremely dangerous."

"I've been over that with Dr. Innis," Neville said. "You're going to have a permanent guard and acid-proof clothing to protect you. That okay?"

"I hope so," Netta said. "I really do!"

XXIII

"How IN HELL did Monty manage to land us without a date this Sunday?" Glenn snapped from the front seat of the van.

"I've *told* you," Bruno sighed. "He held it free in case—"

"In case *Seadeath* was still in the charts and they wanted us for that TV recording," Glenn cut in with a weary air. "I heard you the first time. But he must have known for two weeks at least that they weren't going to."

"Monty's a good manager even if he's not a miracle worker," Bruno said, slowing the van to make the turn into the road to Brindown. "He took a gamble, it didn't work out. And you can't always fix a substitute date on two weeks' notice. I'd have thought you'd be glad of the chance to come back and see if we can lay on this seaside freakout. You were pretty keen on it when we came before, weren't you?"

"Quit wrangling, you two," Cress said from between them. "We talked it over and we agreed, didn't we?"

"Right," Rupert White put in. "Much more of this and I'll start thinking I've wasted my day coming along with you lot." He craned past Gideon, who was obliviously reading as usual, to look out of the back window at the signpost they were passing. "Brindown and—where's the other place? I didn't quite manage to read the name."

"Must have been Coastley," Bruno said. "That's the only other place you get to along this road."

161

"And what's that like?"

"Oh—fishing port, mainly, seaside resort, small holiday camp. And the terminus for a private steamer service that goes to Denmark, I think. It's the port that services Radio Jolly Roger. Haven't you been out there to do any interviews for them?"

"Nope." Rupert twisted his immense length into a slightly more comfortable position, apologizing to Liz for shoving her.

"Funny. Thought you had. Gid and I came down once last winter, and it was an awful trip out from shore with the launch bobbing like a bloody cork— Ah, that's the chemical works. Can't be far now."

He accelerated. Rounding the next bend, he had to clamp his brakes on so violently he almost spilled the passengers from their seats. Gideon, alarmed, complained, but as he raised his eyes and saw the reason, he fell silent.

"That's the way down to our beach!" Nancy burst out.

"Not ours," Bruno muttered, letting the van roll at walking pace.

Parked beside the gate into the field which they had crossed to reach the sea, there was a police car, leaving barely room for the van to squeeze by. Over its roof, beyond the gate, they saw three or four men in dark trousers and blue uniform shirts talking with a man in a light gray suit, as though receiving instructions.

"What in hell can they want?" Glenn demanded.

"I'll make a guess," Bruno said after a pause. "Remember that sergeant came all the way to London to ask about the old lady we met here? Well, maybe something bad has happened to her."

"I didn't see anything in the paper," Gideon muttered.

"You will, if that horrible reporter gets to hear of it," Bruno said. "So what do we do?"

"Save it for another time," Glenn said positively.

"Hell, you mean we came all this way for nothing?" Rupert exclaimed from behind him, sounding annoyed.

"Unless you want to argue with the fuzz," Bruno said. "Shall I go on, and look for a place to turn around, or what?"

"Blazes, having come this far ..." Rupert hunched forward. "Let's at least give ourselves a reason for the trip, hm? Let's go on to Margate or somewhere and have a bathe, maybe!"

"Any other opinions?" Bruno inquired, and when he heard muttered agreement drove on.

They passed the lane leading to the research station, then arrived at a crossroads, from which one road was signposted to Brindown proper, one to Margate by way of Coastley, and one to Margate direct on the main road they had left to follow this lane.

"Which way?" Bruno demanded.

"Go through Coastley," Cress said. "We can wave to Radio Jolly Roger, can't we?"

Bruno complied. A short distance further on, they passed a youngish man with dark hair, trudging along the road in a white coat and dark trousers. He slowed the van.

"Think he wants a lift?" he said.

"We haven't room to give anyone a lift!" Rupert said in annoyance. "Baby, if you pack anything else in here except maybe a chick for me to cuddle, I shall get furious!"

"Okay," Bruno sighed.

"Crazy!" Rupert went on, peering out the back window. "Dr. Kildare on the loose, hm?"

"What do you mean?" Nancy tried to see out past him but his mop of red hair was in the way.

"Oh, just that jacket he was wearing. Sort of a doctor's

oufit, by the look of it. Funny! Not what you'd expect to find on a country lane like this. But kind of smart."

"Hot," Gideon grunted, settling back to his magazine.

Coastley was a small town, barely a dot on the map, but today being a fine summer Sunday it was full of traffic. Bruno had to ease the van very slowly through the main street; unlike Brindown, it was not so small that it fitted in between the road and the sea. He was waiting at a red light when a car about to drive across on the other street suddenly began to hoot vigorously.

"What does he want?" Bruno muttered. He was annoyed at the frustration of their plan to examine the beach in daylight, especially since he had gone to some trouble to persuade Rupert to come along on this trip, sure that he could come up with some spectacular sonic effects with the built-in echo of the chalk cliffs to assist him.

To the fury of drivers behind him, the man from the other car jumped out and waved frantically at Bruno. Recognizing him, Bruno said, "Christ, it's that reporter who was so bloody nasty to me in the police station! Are these lights never going to change? I don't want to talk to him, that's for certain!"

But Leigh-Warden scrambled back in his car, made the turn that took him around the corner and on to the road they must follow across the intersection, and jumped out again just as the lights turned green for them. Sighing, Bruno pulled in to the side of the street as the reporter came running up to the van—if it could be called running; he was too fat to manage much speed.

"What in hell do you want?" Bruno said as rudely as he could. "Your dirty little mind landed us in a mess of trouble last time we came down your way! Know that?"

Leigh-Warden looked abject. He said, in quite a different tone from what Bruno remembered after their first meeting, "Yes, I do owe you an apology for that. I jumped to a conclusion, I'm afraid. Look, can we have a few minutes' chat? I may have something for you, I think—something profitable—and I'm damned certain I can at least tell you something you ought to know."

Bruno hesitated, while the others in the van stared at Leigh-Warden so intensely that he began to flush ever redder than sun and excessive beer-drinking had already made him. He said wearily, "Okay. But I'm blocking traffic. Let me find a place to pull in."

"There's a bus stop down there." Leigh-Warden pointed. "You can use that for five minutes, probably. I'll join you."

Bruno pulled ahead, to the relief of cars behind him which he had been holding up, and Leigh-Warden came trotting and puffing along.

"Not so young as I was once!" he panted. "Ah—well, the good news first. I went up to see a friend of mine who runs a holiday camp between here and Margate—that's why I'm here—and he's just had a pop group booking canceled. He was going to have the Sceneshifters in for a week. Know them?"

"Yes, of course," Bruno said, and from the back of the van Gideon chimed in.

"Because their lead guitarist broke his hand, hm? I heard about that!"

"He's in a tizzy," Leigh-Warden said. "I promised I'd try and find out who your agent is and contact you. From next Friday for a week. Could you manage it? In confidence, he'd willingly pay through the nose—this is a new policy for him, booking pop groups, and it's sold his camp out for the rest of the season, so he daren't not find somebody else!"

"Thanks," Bruno said reluctantly. "I think we might be able to make that, if the terms are right. I'll get our manager to contact him in the morning. What's the name of the place?"

"Here, I brought one of his cards." Leigh-Warden fished it from his pocket, looking triumphant.

"It'd mean canceling the booking at Swanage," Glenn said.

"Yes, but a week's residency wouldn't come amiss after all this traipsing around," Liz countered. "Believe me!"

"I hoped you'd say that," Leigh-Warden beamed. "Maybe it will help to make up for my jumping to the wrong conclusion, as I said." He leaned confidentially on Bruno's door. "You see— My God, what's *that*?"

He shot out his arm, pointing waveringly at a half-seen object stuck to the van's dash with adhesive tape. At the same moment, a couple of giggling thirteen-year-old boys who had been plucking up their courage called from the other side of the van, "Hey, can we have your autographs?"

"Oh, Lord," Bruno muttered. "Well, if we travel around like this . . . Cress, be a love and forge mine for me, will you?"

Glenn, scowling more than was good for the group's image, took the kids' autograph books in through the window and found a pen.

"This?" Bruno went on, tapping it. "Why, it's a mask that Cress made. Modeled after the man we saw come out of the sea the night we—ah—met each other. Remember?"

Leigh-Warden was staring at it as though hypnotized. He said finally, "But it's the spitting image of the missing pilot they were looking for after the crash!"

"Except for *that*," Bruno said, jerking it loose to display the ghastly bare-bone gap in the cheek of the mask.

By now two or three other kids, including two girls, had arrived at the side of the van and Glenn was signing a wrist for one of the girls, a task he seemed to enjoy a little more than merely writing his name on a bit of paper.

"You watch yourself, Glenn Salmon!" Liz said half-seriously from the back. "I've told you before about chicks just out of the shell, haven't I?"

Bruno ignored the banter. He said sharply to Leigh-Warden, "So what surprises you so much about this mask, hm?"

"I . . ." The portly man pulled out a handkerchief and wiped his face. "Well, it's going to be terribly difficult to explain, I'm afraid. This puts an entirely new complexion on the case."

He tucked the handkerchief away, still staring at the mask. "You say this is how the man looked who—?"

"Who came out of the sea when we were having our picnic," Bruno snapped. "Yes! So what, apart from him looking like the lost pilot?"

"Well, all sorts of things have happened since then," the reporter muttered. "You probably know they suspect that he managed to do in the barmy old woman who lived in the Warrinder farm?"

"Yes, we met her. And Sergeant Branksome came to see us in London the next day. But I got the impression she'd just wandered off because she'd set her home on fire. I mean, there wasn't anything in the papers about her being—being murdered or anything."

By now the others had gathered what subject they were discussing; they paused in their autograph signing, heads up and alert.

"That's exactly it!" Leigh-Warden said. "She can't have been. She was found wandering and taken to a mental home. But since then, all kinds of other weird things have been happening in this district. I heard only yesterday that some top-secret consignment was taken to the marine research station. Normally at weekends that's on standby, with no one there except somebody to look after the—the fish stock, or whatever. Feed it, I suppose; *I* don't know! And I tried to talk to the doctor in charge at the hospital and practically got my nose bitten off for my pains. And today the weirdest thing of all—well, actually it broke yesterday, but I didn't catch up with it because I was following up something else—today, anyway, half the police in Kent are being recalled from leave and they're hunting for a man in a male nurse's outfit. I have this horrible feeling that I'm sitting on the biggest story which has broken here since the year one, and I can't pin the bloody thing down!"

There was a dead silence inside the van. One of the kids who had passed in an autograph book said plaintively, "Hey, are you going to be much longer?" They ignored him.

At length Gideon said, "But we saw someone like that. On the way here. Just walking along the road toward this town, whatever it's called."

"What?" Leigh-Warden exclaimed. "How long ago?"

"Ten minutes, maybe," Bruno said. "Look, what do they want this man for, anyhow?"

Leigh-Warden was almost frantic with excitement, but he controlled himself long enough to answer.

"They won't say! All they've told me or the public is that they want to interview him urgently and anybody who sees him must report it. I think it's at least a murder, and I can only assume they haven't yet got the definite evidence. Here, quick—turn around and let's go back to where you saw him! Come on!"

He dashed for his own car.

XXIV

BUT THERE WAS no sign of the dark young man in his white medical coat when they drove back along the road the way they had just come. Either he had made such good progress that he was able to lose himself among the crowd of summer visitors on the outskirts of the town, or he had left the road altogether.

Hooting and waving them to follow, Leigh-Warden led them in his car back to the gate beyond which they had seen the searching police. He stopped, jumped out, and went to the gate while Bruno and his companions waited in their van, exchanging worried glances.

"If that man we saw come out of the sea really has murdered someone . . . ," Liz said softly.

"Be glad it wasn't you, baby," Glenn said cynically.

"Shut up," Bruno said, and craned out of his window. He saw Leigh-Warden beckoning to someone out of sight; then Branksome appeared, not looking too pleased on recognizing the reporter, accompanied by a shirt-sleeved constable; then they talked for a moment and came hurrying toward the van.

"You saw someone answering the description of a male nurse?" Branksome rapped. "On the Coastley road—that right?"

"Yes, about a quarter of an hour ago at most," Bruno said.

"Got that?" Branksome said to the constable.

"I'll radio it in right away, Sarge," the man said, and headed toward the parked police car.

"But that's not all, sergeant," Leigh-Warden said. "Show him the mask, Mr. Twentyman, please."

Silently Bruno complied. Branksome took it and turned it around in his hands. He said, "But the picture was in the papers anyway. . . ." The words trailed away doubtfully. Coming to a sudden decision, he briskened.

"I think Chief Inspector Neville ought to hear about this, anyway. It sounds slim, but a slim chance is better than nothing in a situation like this."

"What *are* you up to, sergeant?" Leigh-Warden probed. "*Is* it murder? I can't see what else would make you mount a search on this scale."

Branksome gave him a level glare. "No, I don't think you could possibly call it murder," he said, and added to Bruno, "The chief inspector is at the marine research station. You know it?"

"Yes, we found our way there last time we came down here."

"I'll see you there in a few minutes, then."

"But, 'Reen—!" Sellers said desperately to the phone, casting around for a fresh argument. He hit on one, and said in a pleading voice, "Look, didn't you say yourself, just the other day, that my job really is the way you see on telly and the pictures—having to sort of be on duty even when officially you aren't?"

She sniffed, as though dismissing that as a valid excuse for calling off their next date.

"I can't help it!" he exclaimed. He looked around him nervously; he was in an office at the end of the corridor he was supposed to be guarding, and he had just caught a faint noise outside. He craned to the window as far as the phone's cord would allow, and went on talking. "Marty

Swires is in the same predicament as me, and so's Phil Paitch—we've all been told to come here and . . . Oh-oh! 'Reen, I'll have to ring off. My sergeant just turned up, and—Lord, it's Bruno and his group, coming this way! Hey, if you want a chance to meet them, why don't you hop on your bike and come over, hm?"

He didn't have time to hear her answer, but hastily put down the phone and stepped back into the passage, just in time to turn with a bored-looking expression and greet Branksome as he opened the external door and peered in.

"Is Mr. Neville here?" he demanded.

"No, sarge. He's with the scientists over in the main lab. Mrs. Reedwall came to fetch the others about five minutes ago." He didn't add that that was what had given him the opportunity of calling his girl-friend.

The whole situation he had got caught up in was a complete mystery to him still. Exactly why one of the male nurses from Geddesley Mental Hospital—he had a good eye for faces and had recognized the prisoner at once—should be locked up in a marine research station while the scientific staff flapped back and forth like frightened chickens, he couldn't guess, and since he was called in to act as temporary guard no one in authority had stopped long enough in his vicinity for him to put the question.

Sighing, he returned to the chair they had put outside the door of the constant-temperature room and tried to interest himself in the book he had brought to pass the time. Apparently he was going to have to spend the night here as well, on a camp bed, and he didn't fancy that in the least.

Scowling, Chief Inspector Neville looked up from the eyepiece of the microscope to which Netta had called her colleagues' attention. What he had just seen meant nothing to him, and he was beginning to feel a little embarrassed at having to take the scientists' word on something that seemed so utterly fantastic. The courage that had enabled him to beard the Assistant Chief Constable and persuade him to turn on a full-scale search for the pseudo-Stevens on the pretext that a hypothetical maniac had made away with Miss Beeding and stolen the male nurse's clothing by way of disguise was now wearing thin, and he was starting to wonder whether in the cold light of a Monday morning he would see the perfectly rational explanation for these alarming events that at present was eluding him.

The appearance of Branksome was a relief; this heralded a police matter, something he understood and could cope with. His tone was cordial as he greeted the visitor.

"Sir, it sounds as though the man we're looking for has been spotted on the Coastley road," Branksome said. "About—oh—twenty minutes ago. I've already had a report radioed in to county HQ and they promised to get a car there as fast as possible. But that's not the only thing that's come up. There's something else which is—well—peculiar. . . ."

He explained rapidly about the encounter Bruno and his group had had with a man from the sea. Standing just inside the doorway of the lab, having exchanged nods with Tom Reedwall, they were staring at the dissected specimen on the table and all the complex scientific equipment in use to study it.

It was clear from Neville's expression that he did not approve of wild stories like this, especially from way-out young people involved with a pop group; even Cress's explanation of the way she had designed the mask seemed to leave him cold. But Tom and Netta were impressed and made no attempt to hide it.

"Bruno!" Tom exclaimed. "Let's have that again. The man came out of the water—would you say 'reluctantly'?"

"Exactly!" Liz answered before Bruno could speak. "When I first saw him, I mistook him for an injured dog."

"That fits," Netta said. "If this was the—the first in-crossing, so to speak, of land-going memories into the creature's experience ... And you say he wasn't breathing?"

"Literally," Bruno confirmed. "I must have had my arm around him for twenty paces, and someone in that condition ought to have been gasping for air."

"Then when he fell over," Glenn supplied, "a bloody great torrent of water poured out of his mouth. Ugh!"

"It all fits!" Tom said, pounding fist into palm. "It found the body of the drowned pilot before any significant decomposition set in, took it over, and was gradually impelled toward the land by these new memories it had acquired, but when it got to shore it had a hell of a struggle digesting the contradiction between its own experience and the new prey's, and it kept going on dissolved oxygen in the water it held until it accidentally spilled this reserve and had to start using air instead. Lord, that must have been painful—raw dry air on its new internal tissues!"

"If it feels pain in any sense we can recognize," Dr. Innis put in. He looked very tired; neither he nor the Reedwalls had managed more than a snatch of sleep last night. "I don't see how it can. In an evolutionary sense, damage to the body of the prey can only matter insofar as it hinders pursuit of a fresh victim."

"Why do you keep saying 'it,' and not 'he'?" Cress said.

There was a taut pause. Branksome broke it by saying to Neville, "I think we owe these people an explanation, sir. If we'd been a little more ready to listen when they first reported what they'd seen, we might have saved Miss Beeding, and Stevens, and Ryan's hand."

"All right," Neville agreed, and turned to Tom. "Will you sum it up?"

When Tom had finished, they were dazed.

"Christ, I suggested offering it a lift!" Bruno exploded. "And right back when we first saw it, we planned to take it to hospital in the van!"

Gideon said nothing, but looked at his hands as though imagining how it would feel to suffer as Ryan had suffered. There was another pause.

"Very clear, Dr. Reedwall!" a mocking voice said. "Congratulations!"

They all started, and swung around to find the source of the words. Peering in through one of the lab's open windows, unnoticed until now, was Leigh-Warden, pen and notebook in hand, the pages of the latter closely covered with a shorthand transcription of everything Tom had said.

On the point of shouting at him, Neville changed his mind and looked deflated. He said, "And what exactly do you think you're going to do with the fruits of your eavesdropping?"

"I'll give you three guesses," Leigh-Warden smiled.

"Precisely nothing," Neville said. "You've just made my mind up for me. I've been stalling on this for a day and a half, but listening to what Dr. Reedwall was saying has finally tipped the balance. You won't get *that* into print."

"How are you going to stop me?" Leigh-Warden countered, but he sounded alarmed.

"This thing is too damned dangerous to be handled the way we've tried up to now," Neville said. "I'm going to risk everything. I'm going straight to a phone. I'm going to call in troops, and even if I have to lie to do it I'm going to have this business put under a D notice or anything else

I can think of. You can call it a murder hunt if you like—that'll worry people, and nothing more. But you put a single word of the real facts into print, and you'll start a panic. Not that that would bother you, would it? Panics make good copy, too!"

Framed in the window, Leigh-Warden's face went quite dead, as though he too had been taken over by a nonhuman creature. He said at last, "Damn you. *Damn* you! I know I've made a bloody mess of my life! I know I've wound up a second-rater! But why do bastards like you get so much pleasure out of rubbing my bloody nose in it? Here!"

With sudden violence he hurled the notebook across the room, its leaves flapping like frantic multiple wings.

"There, have it back! Go on—it's a present from me! It's only the biggest damned story I ever ran across in my life, the last one that could haul me out of this foul backwater town! But—"

He drew a deep breath, while his audience stared in embarrassment at seeing him stripped thus psychologically naked.

"But what I hate most about you smug bastards is that you're right, aren't you? And I know it. I even admit it sometimes. So for the sake of the poor devils who scrape the other fifty weeks of the year to rent a caravan facing the beach, for the sake of the kids who look forward to their holiday for months, for all those horrible little people out there who'd scatter and run or lock their doors and think every stranger and maybe some of their friends were monsters—have it back! Burn it! Do what the hell you like with it!"

And he concluded almost in a whisper: "But if this thing isn't caught with all your troops and coppers before the next time it wants to eat and change, if it gets at someone else who could have been told the truth and wasn't because *you* didn't want to start a panic—God have mercy on your soul, Neville, because I never shall."

He swung on his heel, and a moment later there was the sound of his car's door slamming and the engine blasting into life.

XXV

IT WAS A very young and rather nervous lieutenant who greeted Neville on his arrival at the headquarters of the 19th/99th Kentish Bombardiers, "The Hop-Pickers"— a former stately home taken over during World War II by the War Office and retained to give the regiment a permanent base in its own county. He listened with great gravity to Neville's hurried explanation, then posed two questions which showed he had at least grasped the essence of the problem.

"Is this man dangerous?" he demanded.

"We think he may be," Neville said, and added the lie he had been debating in the car all the way here: "He is quite likely to throw acid at anyone attempting to arrest him."

"Hmmm!" the very young lieutenant said, obviously wishing this of all weekends had not been his turn on duty. "And have you pictures of him?"

"I'm having Identikit drawings prepared at the moment. They ought to be ready for distribution in a couple of hours."

"Well, in that case ..." the lieutenant sighed, and reached for a phone. "Guard room? Ah, corporal! Duty officer here. We've had an appeal from the police for assistance in a hunt for a suspected murderer. Turn out the guard and have them muster everyone you can rope in, please!"

The hot Sunday evening lay heavy on the North Kent coast. The roads back toward London began to fill with home-bound traffic. On every road leading out of the area between Geddesley and Coastley, children whined in traffic jams while their parents complained furiously about the holdup caused by police inspection of every single vehicle. The stench of exhaust gases gathered almost visibly above the hordes of delayed cars and the proprietors of petrol stations rubbed their hands and chortled as they calculated how much fuel was going to waste.

What Neville had called Identikit drawings were not as strictly official as he had led the young lieutenant to believe. Bruno and the group had been asked to go to Geddesley police station—larger than Brindown's, and better equipped—to make a statement about what they had seen on the beach a short eternity ago, and there they had found a harassed Dr. Nimms trying to compose a portrait of Stevens under the guidance of a recently recruited detective who was as yet not very good with the Identikit equipment.

He was just about ready to blow his top at the inadequacy of his visual memory when Cress helped herself to a sheet of paper and a pencil and started sketching. She mutely held out the result for him to see.

"Now that's a bit more like it!" he exclaimed, thrusting aside the detective's latest effort and seizing Cress's. "Except his chin was a bit plumper—" Suddenly realizing who he was talking to, he said, "Who on earth are you?"

"Never mind!" the detective said, with an approving glance at Cress in today's ultra-short minidress of brilliant red, yellow, and black. "All that matters is to get a picture of this bod out to the people searching for him!"

Plying an eraser, Cress paid no attention.

A small van bearing on its sides the legend CON-TRACT SECURITY GUARD SERVICE LTD. halted at a red light in Coastley prior to turning down the road which led to the small harbor. It was far too hot to have the windows up, in driver Pete Morley's view, but that led to problems, and one appeared now in the shape of an excited small girl on the pavement, reaching out her hand and exclaiming, "Ooh, what a *big* dog!"

Beside Pete on the passenger seat, Ajax gave a warning growl and his hackles rose.

"Don't touch!" Pete said sharply. "He's a trained guard dog—won't allow anybody near the van!"

"Lissa! Come away from there!" the girl's mother called, and with a rebellious glare the child departed. Ajax relaxed.

"All right for you, boy," Pete sighed. "You don't know how late we are, do you? Bob's going to be furious!"

The light changed to green. He accelerated around the bend toward the port.

There was comparatively little seaborne traffic through Coastley, but some of the freight that passed via the docks was quite valuable and easy enough to dispose of to tempt thieves—mainly Scandinavian furniture and textiles, which were brought in by the little local steamer line to Copenhagen. For four or five years past, since a big theft in which the raiders got clean away with eight thousand pounds' worth of loot, the owners of the line had staked the port to a night security service. Today, Pete and Ajax were that service.

"But the kid was right," Pete muttered as he hooted to be let through the gate. "You're a beautiful beast, aren't you?"

The gigantic Alsatian beside him gave panting approval to the compliment.

"And where the hell have you been?" Bob Cole said, appearing from the harbormaster's office to let them in.

"Sorry," Pete explained. "There's some kind of a manhunt going on, I think—police are holding up traffic on all the roads near here."

"Well, you're not likely to come to any harm with that thing to help out," Bob shrugged. "All right, move it along—I want to get home to my supper."

Gradually, car by car, the monstrous five-mile jams caused by the police check dispersed, although the watch on the roads continued. Night crept slowly on, and a little cloud drifted up from the west, concealing the moon.

Dismayed by what they had stumbled into, Bruno and his companions were finally allowed to leave the police station at Geddesley, having been questioned and requestioned by detectives who clearly did not believe a word of what they had been told. Emerging into the street, heading back to where they had parked the van, Glenn said loudly, "I guess you're as sick of this damn-fool business as I am, aren't you?"

"What hurts me, man," Gideon said when it was clear that none of the others wanted to answer, "is the way that poor bloody reporter broke up!"

"Him!" Glenn spat ostentatiously into the gutter. "He didn't give a damn what harm he was doing to us when he printed that story in the papers the other day! Well, did he?"

"No, but today . . ." Bruno said, and the words died.

"I tell you one thing definite," Cress said, her voice as determined as her small pretty face. "I'd like to stick around here for a bit and see how things develop. That scientist at the research station—Tom—seems like a nice guy, and I'm sure he wouldn't mind if we called back there."

Bruno checked his watch. "A bit late now," he said dubiously. "And anyway, I'd like a drink, and something to eat."

"But let's stay over," Cress suggested. "We want to follow up that holiday-camp date, don't we?"

"I can fix that by calling Monty. But the hell, let's do it. Everybody think it's a good idea?"

"Sure," Gideon shrugged. "If we can find somewhere to sleep in this overcrowded district. It's peak holiday time, remember."

"Hell, we can sleep in the van if we have to," Liz said. "Let's go get that drink—I'm parched!"

Grumbling to one another, but pleased in an upside-down kind of way to find a use for the training they had been drilled through, men of the Kentish Bombardiers deployed around the area as though in preparation for a battle. It was only the sergeants and warrant officers, who had been to the main briefing conducted by Chief Inspector Neville, who knew about—and were worried about—something that had cropped up almost in passing.

As soon as the equipment could be laid on, perhaps in the small hours of tomorrow morning, as many of their men as possible were going to be issued with protective clothing. What did that mean? They knew of such gear only in the context of exercises simulating the use of nuclear weapons. One could half-suspect that news had come of an impending H-bomb attack, or an invasion under cover of tactical nukes.

But the sergeants and WO's shrugged it off. They had been in the army long enough to leave the real thinking to their officers; meantime, they had nearly a hundred

grousing men to cope with, all resentful at being called out
from their barracks on a hot summer Sunday evening.

It was nearly midnight when they finally decided that
they had drawn a blank in looking for accommodation.
Extremely glum, Bruno and the group exchanged glances
inside the van.

"Well?" Rupert White said, and when no one answered, went on, "Well, I tell you what I'm going to do.
I'm going home—even if I have to hitch!"

"There's one last train," Liz said. "I looked at a time-
table when we were checking that hotel."

"Great! Coming with me, then?"

Liz hesitated. Then she shook her head. "No, I want to
stick around. Like I said, I'd cheerfully sleep in the van."

"Where? You can't simply park in the street, can you?"

"How about at the marine research station?" Cress
suggested. "I bet they wouldn't mind if we parked in their
little lane."

"That's an idea," Bruno said with a nod. "The Reedwalls are pretty friendly—they'd let us wash in their
house, I guess, and use the loo. Might even give us some
breakfast tomorrow."

"Me, I don't believe all of this," Rupert said. "But if it
is true, I'd rather be a good few miles away. And if it's
not, I'll have the pleasure of laughing at you. Bruno, drop
me at the station, will you?"

"What's that?" Netta exclaimed, raising her fair head
from the eyepiece of the microscope. The latest of perhaps
two hundred specimens was on the stage. By now, the
dead creature was practically reduced to its skeleton.
Across in the building that contained the constant-
temperature room, with Sellers watching, Dr. Innis was

making notes of the live creature's appearance and behavior.

"What's what?" Tom demanded, depositing in a sample jar an organ that was neither swim-bladder nor lung, but partook of the nature of both.

"I heard a noise at the window—oh!"

She started, then laughed as the window was drawn back to reveal Gideon's dark face.

"Hey! Sorry to surprise you—did you think I was that plastic Dr. Kildare they're looking for? But we saw the lights on, and . . ."

He explained what he and the group wanted, and both Netta and Tom shrugged.

"Sure, why not?" Tom said. "I don't think anyone will mind."

"Thanks," Gideon said, and vanished to report the good news.

It was nearly dawn when Pete set off on his fifth tour of the stacked bales, crates, and cartons along the dockside at Coastley. Armed with a truncheon, a flashlight, and his dog, he went cautiously. It was an eerie setting even on a summer night: the still, dark forms of the two freighters lying to, the skeletal shapes of the dockside cranes like vast metallic mantises.

They had almost completed the tour, without incident, when Ajax suddenly cocked his ears and growled. Pete tensed. Abruptly the dog hurled himself forward, into a patch of total darkness between two tall stacks of crates.

Pete darted after him, but dared not go into the narrow gap. He shone his torch and shouted, hoping to bolt the thieves—if thieves they were—and saw nothing. Warily he circled the nearer of the two high stacks, and came to the other side of the gap between them. Bewildered, he saw and heard nothing now. He called Ajax, expecting the answering growl he was accustomed to; then he picked his way along the gap, truncheon ready, and came out the other side astonished and dismayed.

He had not even noticed the soft heap of—*something*—that lay against the left-hand stack of crates.

Eventually he decided, angrily, that Ajax had broken training for the first time ever, and went off on a vain search of the docks, shouting for him.

XXVI

"LORD! IT'S NEARLY nine o'clock!" Tousle-haired, Netta rolled out of bed, with a jab at Tom's ribs. He roused, resentfully, then also swung his feet to the floor as he remembered what had happened and why it was imperative not to waste time sleeping. Monday today—they could expect help from outside, have this appalling burden taken off their limited resources. . . .

"That poor policeman!" Netta said, thrusting her feet into slippers. "I bet he didn't spend a very good night. I'll put some coffee on and go and see if he'd like some, okay?"

She gathered a robe about her and was gone, leaving Tom to stumble to the washbasin and wake himself with cold water.

"What in the world . . . ?"

Sam Fletcher rounded the last bend in the lane before the gate to the grounds in which the research station stood, and braked abruptly. Parked at the point where the lane widened just before the gate, there stood the incredibly painted van of Bruno and the Hermetic Tradition.

"The nerve!" he muttered, getting out to open the gate and let his car through. "Who do they think they are, using this land as though they owned it?"

He marched over to the van and peered in through the windscreen. Miniature curtains were drawn over the side windows, but enough light filtered in for him to see sleeping forms stretched out on the bunks and one across the bench-seat in front: a pretty girl who had taken off her dress to use as a coverlet, then lost it when she turned over during the night.

"Bloody shameless," he muttered. For an instant he considered thumping on the window; then he changed his mind. Better to bring the full force of Dr. Innis' authority down on them.

"Next thing you know," he said to the air, "we'll have a bloody caravan site interfering with the work here!"

He marched back to the car, via the gate to open it, and drove to his usual parking place. Jumping out, he looked around. The Reedwalls' bedroom curtains were still drawn—something he had never seen before as late as nine o'clock, even on a Monday.

He strode toward Dr. Innis's office, rapped, and received no reply. Anxious not to miss the chance of telling off the people sleeping in the van, he searched the entire premises, coming finally to the incubation building that contained the constant-temperature room. There he stopped dead. Ahead of him there stood a rumpled camp bed.

"The cheek!" he exclaimed. "The bloody nerve! Using our buildings as a hotel, are they?"

He strode up to the bed and kicked it over, fuming. At the noise, there was a movement beyond the door of the constant-temperature room, and he tensed.

"Gone in there?" he wondered. "Well, that's *too* much, damn it! That's the absolute bloody limit!"

He seized the handle of the door. It seemed to be stuck. After a moment he realized it was locked, and tugged a chain of keys from his pocket—those that were issued to all the staff, but seldom used.

Thrusting the key home and turning it, he flung the door open and marched in.

"Now you listen to me!" he snapped. "You haven't any right to—"

"This is very kind of you," Sellers said gratefully as he sipped the hot coffee Netta had prepared and crunched on his second piece of toast. "Must say, it wasn't much fun trying to sleep in that corridor, with—with whatever it is the other side of the door."

He hesitated. "What is it, anyway?" he demanded.

"That's what we're trying to find out," Tom muttered, pouring himself some coffee and coming to join Sellers at table. "Whatever it is, though, it definitely isn't human." And he added, while Sellers was struggling with that astonishing remark, "Darling, why don't you see if the people in the van want some breakfast, too? I don't imagine they had a very comfortable night, either."

Netta appeared from the bedroom, wriggling her dress down over her hips. "Yes, I'll go and ask—but by this time of morning, of course, they may just have woken up and driven off."

She headed for the door. Tom called after her. "Hey! See if there's any sign of Doc Innis, will you?"

"Okay!" she called back, and was gone.

"Dr. Reedwall, you did say that thing wasn't human, didn't you?" Sellers ventured.

"Yes, it appears to be some kind of fish," Tom agreed. "With the power to adopt other forms more or less at will."

"You mean that's what all this big search is about?" Sellers exclaimed. "Is that what happened to—?"

Netta interrupted him, flinging the door open again. Her face was very pale.

"Tom, quickly! Sam's car is parked outside and there's no sign of him anywhere! He doesn't know about the shapechanger. I just realized we forgot to call him when he got home last night!"

Liz sat up on the front seat of the van and pulled her dress over her head. "Hey, you lot!" she shouted. "It's nine o'clock and someone just came to look into the van. Shake a leg there!"

Behind her the others awoke, grumbling, pulling on their clothes. Eeling over the side of his top bunk to give Nancy a good-morning kiss, Gideon prodded Glenn in the ribs—he had lost the series of tosses to decide who must have the floor in the middle of the van—and within minutes they were all fit to face the world, though still yawning and stretching.

"Hey, there's Netta," Bruno said, clambering over the back of the driver's seat to let himself out. "Think they'd give us a cup of coffee or something? What in the world—?"

They all saw what he meant: Netta frantically beckoning Tom to follow her, and then Rodge Sellers wiping his face with a handkerchief and running at the same time. They caught a wordless, terrified cry.

"Something's wrong!" Bruno exclaimed. "Gid—Glenn —move it! Let's see if we can help!"

"Oh, my God," Tom said, halting before the half-open door of the constant-temperature room. Then, as Netta came up behind, he thrust her away and slammed it. "No use!" he snapped. "And don't think you'd learn anything by looking either! All there is in there is a kind of—of puddle!"

Netta stared at him blankly. During the silence, Sellers said in a puzzled voice, "I'm sure I didn't knock the bed over like that."

"Sam?" Netta forced out at last.

"I suppose so," Tom said, very pale, and swallowed hard.

"Oh, my God," Netta whispered. "Oh, my God! Tom, he was a swine, but—but nobody deserves to have that happen to him. Nobody! Nobody!"

She crumpled suddenly against his chest, and over her fair head Tom and Sellers stared at each other, terrified at the actualization of the threat they had known before only at a distance.

As they made to clamber over the closed gate of the research station, a car hooted from behind. Bruno swung around and saw a white-haired head peering from the window of a Rover.

"Who are you? What are you doing?" the driver called.

"Ah—we're friends of Dr. Reedwall," Bruno improvised. "We slept here in our van last night and we were just going to say thank you." He groped in memory for a name. "Are you the—the director? Dr. Innis?"

"That's right. Oh! Are you the young people who actually saw this creature come ashore, the one we have a specimen of?" Innis's manner changed magically as they all nodded.

"Well, then! Come along, let me through the gate! I heard all about this business of yours before I went home last night, and I think you deserve a cup of coffee or something for the information you gave us. I'm sure Mrs. Reedwall— Hello! What's that?"

They turned to follow his gaze, and saw Sellers emerge from one of the buildings, calling and waving to them.

"Something's wrong, sir," Bruno muttered. "We saw the Reedwalls in a big panic a moment ago."

"Well, Sam Fletcher's here now—they oughtn't to have much difficulty in . . ." Innis's voice trailed away. "Oh, Lord! He doesn't know, he doesn't *know*!"

"As far as we can see," Tom explained, "he must have seen the van parked with the people sleeping in it, and come looking for you to tell them off. Sam's like—I mean, he was like that, wasn't he, rather?"

Beside him, red-eyed, Netta struggled to control her horror and dismay.

"And now the other side of that door, there's—there's another *thing* on the way. And this one, if it follows the previous pattern, is going to know everything Sam Fletcher knew. It's got his keys, and the two halves of it taken together will remember how to use them!"

Sellers silently gathered up the protective clothing which had been borrowed from the chemical plant, and started to put it on. He said, "Then someone had better go and get them back while the thing is still a—a puddle. Right?"

Innis looked at him thoughtfully. He said after a pause, "No, take that outfit off, young man. I need it."

"What?" Tom and Netta spoke as one.

"I'm not exactly a chicken any longer, am I? And someone ought to watch the process of reconstruction of the creature from its—its raw material, so to speak. Quick, go to the lab! Specimen slides, containers, tongs, scalpels—anything you can think of!"

He seized the heavy protective clothing from Sellers and thrust his legs into the cumbersome suit. Seeing that Tom and Netta had not responded, he snapped, "Move, damn you!"

"But it's—it's Sam," Netta said faintly.

"You know as well as I do that he was a loathsome example of our species," Innis said. "But he had one saving grace: he was interested in his work, and good at it. If he could offer no other excuse for his life, he could still help to save someone else from the same fate. And we haven't much time. Haven't you seen this morning's papers?"

"N-no," Netta admitted. "We overslept."

"There's a hideously garbled version of this business in at least one of the more sensational rags. I saw it when I stopped for some cigarettes on the way here. Hurry!"

In the background, Glenn curled his lip. "The way that poor reporter broke up!" he quoted at Gideon. "So much for your power to judge human nature! Some show he put on, hm?"

Puzzled and disheartened, Gideon did not attempt to reply.

Last night Leigh-Warden had drunk himself into a stupor; this morning, his mouth was foul and his head ached. He barely made it to the front door of his home to collect the newspapers—he had them all delivered—and the milk. He made a cup of coffee, changed his mind about putting the milk in, and sipped it black as he riffled through the papers. It was in the next-to-last that he came across the garbled story. His mind reeled as he read snatches: "Manhunt by Kent Police . . . Sea monster reported from pirate radio ship . . . Official curtain of silence . . ."

There was no coherent thought in his mind, only reflex, a pattern of ideas he had rehearsed in imagination so many times it required no planning. In the drawer of the desk at which he sat to compile his little sensational snippets about holiday wife-trading, a souvenir of his war service, with bullets.

The last thought he carried to his grave was the ironical reflection that someone who had made his living by condensing people's private tragedies into brief paragraphs ought to leave a suicide note.

But it seemed like too much trouble.

"Right!" Innis said crisply, settling the acid-proof helmet on his head and grasping the sampling tools in his clumsy gauntlets. "Open that door, young man!"

Worried, Tom complied, using his own key. Innis strode through with determination, and the moment he passed the threshold, halted.

"It's gone!" he said. "Lord, it—it's *gone!*"

XXVII

RORY DUNSTABLE HAD hoped not to see this road again for at least three weeks; he was on leave and intended to spend his free time water-skiing and skin diving in the Channel Islands. Late last night he had been stowing all his gear in the car, ready for an early start this morning. There was a girl, working through the summer as a hostess in a Guernsey discothèque. . . .

But she was going to be extremely disappointed today, and possibly tomorrow as well. What he had seen when he went around to the local newsagents to pick up the morning papers had sent him running for the car.

Every now and again he swore at the air, his car racing at the legal limit down the broad eastward highway towards Brindown.

"Gone?" Tom echoed stupidly, and thrust in behind Innis to survey the constant-temperature room.

"You find it!" Innis said savagely, tearing off his helmet. He stepped back, and his booted foot encountered something lying on the floor. He glanced at it, and started.

"That's the grille of the ventilation pipe!" he exclaimed. He dropped on one knee and groped under the lowest shelf.

"Of course, we never thought of that," Netta sighed. "In its plastic state, just after changing, it could sort of pour itself down a pipe like that!"

Tom snapped his fingers. "But this means the creature

is even more dangerous than we thought. It must be able to remember and reason even while it's going through the change process. It must have wanted to get away as soon as possible; it must have realized directly I walked in and found it that its escape would be blocked by the corridor route, and figured out that it could get down that pipe while it was still—well, as I said, still a puddle!"

"How could a puddle tear loose that grille?" Innis demanded. "Mr. Neville made quite sure it was anchored."

"It didn't tear it loose. It—well—it digested it loose." Tom held the metal mesh up; the ends of the bars were scarred with the marks of acid.

"So we've lost it back to the sea," Innis muttered. "Now there's no knowing what innocent person may fall victim to it next time it needs to feed and change."

"No, we haven't," Netta said.

"What?" Innis blinked at her. "But that pipe leads out over the water—has to, to keep the air in here humid."

"Not any longer," Netta said. "At least not over the sea. It leads to the dolphin pens!"

"After it, then!" Innis snapped, and led them in a rush down the corridor.

A little uncertain, Rory drew his car in alongside the Hermetic Tradition's van. He recognized it—it was known to everyone in the pop music industry—and was at a loss to know why it should be here. Then he recalled the vague mention he had heard, during the discussions he had eavesdropped on between Tom and Netta while they were arguing about the curious fish-thing brought in from Organic Acids, of a visit by the group to this part of the country.

He got out, went through the gate, and called out for the Reedwalls or Dr. Innis. Not hearing a reply, he walked right through the station until he rounded the corner of one of the largest buildings and suddenly saw not only the staff scientists, but also Bruno's group, gathered on the edge of a large water-filled pit rimmed with concrete like an overgrown swimming pool.

He called out again. They turned around, and by the looks on their faces Bruno and Gideon, who knew him from their visits to Radio Jolly Roger, were astonished to see him here. Muttering greetings to them, he went directly over to Innis.

"Sir, I think I probably owe you an apology," he said.

"What?" Innis glanced at him, preoccupied.

"Yes." Rory sounded as depressed as he felt. "I was at a party last night, and I got talking to someone I didn't know, and—well, I was a bit drunk, to be honest. And he was interested in fishing, and I started talking more freely than I should have done. And I see from this morning's papers that something has got out about this thing you have here."

"Now which of us was right about that 'bloody reporter'?" Gideon muttered, nudging Glenn, who scowled but held his tongue.

Rory had expected Innis to fly off the handle, but instead the elderly scientist merely sighed. "That's not the only thing that's got out," he muttered. "Look down there and you'll see the things as they are in life instead of laid out on a dissecting table!"

With an awful sensation as though he had just been pitched into a bottomless chasm, Rory turned his attention for the first time to the water in the dolphin pens and there saw, feebly swimming about, two weird creatures like enormously elongated men, as though one were to take a human body and try to force it to resemble an eel.

Swallowing hard as he stared at the appalling deformed

beasts, he said, "But I thought they actually copied people!"

"They're cleverer than that," Innis said somberly. "The only way those two could get out of where we'd imprisoned the—the parent one was down a narrow pipe. And it, or they, gambled on getting away. They didn't quite make it. But all that stopped them was the lucky chance that the final phase of their transformation came too soon, while they were still compelled to stay slender enough to pass through the pipe. Otherwise no doubt they'd have come out as perfect as the other copies."

"I think they're getting stronger," Netta said nervously. "I told Tom right at the start I suspected the change was terribly fast. If we leave them much longer they'll be strong enough to climb out."

"We'll have to trap them, then," Tom said.

"How? They're probably as clever as we are by now, having absorbed not just old Miss Beeding's crazy thoughts but Stevens's and now Sam's as well." Netta gulped, as though talking rationally of Fletcher's fearful fate were still beyond her powers of self-control.

"Nets, I suppose," Tom shrugged.

"But you can't net them if they stay in the middle of the pool, and if you wait until they're fully recovered they may be able to break free and run for it!"

"So we tackle them *before* they're fully recovered," Tom snapped. "Go fetch my scuba kit, quickly!"

"Darling, you—!" Netta paled.

"I'll tackle the other one," Rory said. "I have my scuba in the car. And I'm pretty good at this, though I say it myself."

Innis stepped up between them. "Dr. Reedwall, are you sure you want to do this? Remember, those creatures probably have some of their aquatic memories, too— they'll be far more at home in the water than you are."

"Short of poisoning the pool, what else do you suggest?" Tom rapped. "We have four husky young men to help us hold them once we get them out of the water, and drag them back where they came from—we ought to manage it okay. But if we delay too long, they'll have completely got over the change process. Someone go find some nets for us! Someone block off the outlet of that pipe to stop them trying the same trick twice!"

He was stripping off his shirt as he spoke.

Once the decision was taken, the rest of them forgot their doubts. While Tom and Rory were putting on their scuba gear, watched from the body of the dolphin pen by the two weak but wary shapechangers, Netta took the others briskly in charge, directing Sellers to fetch nets from the shed on the wharf where they were kept—tough webs of green nylon far stronger than a man could tear apart—while the others hunted for wire, hammers, staples, and anything else that might serve to block the end of the ventilation pipe. It was difficult to reach from the side of the pool, but it could be done.

"They must have been too soft to stand up," Netta said with grim humor. "Otherwise they'd never have needed to fall into the water at all!"

When the moment came, the watchers were so tense they hardly dared breathe, but Tom was perfectly matter-of-fact as he dropped over the side of the pool, legs together, net in one hand and a trident harpoon in the other. Sensing, or calculating, what was to be done, the shapechangers had swum to the far end from where the watchers were assembled.

"You, young fellow—you've got a good reach on you!" Innis rapped at Gideon. "Find a pole or something, and if they try to climb out beat 'em back! I've just noticed something that may make all the difference! They're stay-

197

ing at the surface, aren't they? They must have fixed themselves in the air-breathing phase. If they try to breathe water again they may even drown themselves!"

"Yes, of course!" Netta exclaimed, showing the first hint of cheerfulness she had managed since Tom announced his intention of going into the pool after the creatures. "Their memories must be short from one phase to the next, mustn't they? They wouldn't want to start behaving like sharks when they were pretending to be halibut!"

Gideon had taken station at the far side of the pool, armed with a long metal pipe. He gestured at the creatures in the water as though shooing geese, and shouted. Startled, they darted back, and at the same moment Rory joined Tom in the water.

Staring down at the creatures she had called, on the spur of the moment, shapechangers, Netta dug her nails into her palms. It would have been bad enough watching a contest like this without Tom being involved; with him down there, she hardly knew whether to shut her eyes or hold them open with her fingers so as not to miss a single movement.

Like aquatic gladiators, nets spreading out in the water, Rory and Tom closed on their quarry. Without having to consult about it, they hit on the best course immediately: to try and separate them into opposite halves of the pool. Tom feinted with his harpoon at the nearer creature, and it darted back. Rory copied him, and his darted in the same direction. For a while there was only that silent maneuvering, like the opening of a chess game where each player warily forestalls his opponent's traps.

Suddenly, without warning, one of the creatures plunged at Rory. He spun in the water and thrust out his harpoon. The creature's flesh seemed to absorb it, shedding no blood, and its vastly elongated arms encircled him, seeking to pull off his breathing mask. He stabbed vainly, again and again, and without effect.

Meantime Tom seized his chance and dived headfirst at the other creature. At the last moment before collision, he swerved aside like a matador and left his net in the creature's path. The instant there was contact, he kicked frantically toward the bottom, dragging the creature with him. Its limbs hampered by the net, he calculated that it stood no chance of drawing him to the surface, and if he held it under long enough, breathing with his mask, it must either drown or risk the change to a water-breathing phase, which would trap it effectively anyway, here in the dolphin pen.

Turning, triumphant, he saw with horror that Rory was in difficulties. For a single heartbeat he came close to letting go the net he clutched. Then reason prevailed. He could not go to the rescue for fear of releasing his own captive, and then it in turn might attack him.

Alarmed, he saw how the creature clawing at Rory was managing to turn the tables, dragging him toward the side of the pool, its eel-thin legs flailing the water well out of reach of Rory's and much more powerful.

Then, suddenly, the creature stiffened and jerked like a frog's leg on a galvanic plate, and Rory seized his chance. He broke free and frantically tangled his own net around the creature, leaving it to flail around while he stood off out of reach and discouraged its attempts to grab him again with jabs of his trident.

Tom strained to see what had saved Rory's bacon, and suddenly recognized it, lying on the bottom: the length of pipe Gideon had taken in hand, hurled down like a javelin the instant the creature broke the surface.

After that, it was a matter of waiting. Within five minutes, the churning and thrashing in the nets ceased, and with an exchange of nods he and Rory swam with their captives to the side of the pool, where Sellers and the members of the Hermetic Tradition seized them, dragged them out, and carted them off to be locked up again in the prison from which they had so brilliantly escaped. And this time the exit to the pool was sealed.

They were still busy with compliments and congratulations, Netta kissing Tom with shining eyes, Rory trying to make Gideon accept proper thanks in face of a barrage of shrugs and half-embarrassed disclaimers, when there was the noise of another car approaching. Around the corner Chief Inspector Neville appeared, face like thunder, calling loudly for Dr. Innis.

Innis hurried over to him, while the others fell silent one by one and wondered what could have happened. Half under her breath, Netta said, "I never thought—oh, God! If the one we had here needed to eat and change this morning, then someone else must have been taken, by the one which is still at large!"

They hastened to join Innis and Neville, demanding to know whether there had indeed been another victim.

"Another victim?" Neville snapped. "Me! That's all! I've been arguing with the Chief Constable since half-past eight, because I called out the army and laid on road blocks yesterday! I'm going to be carpeted, the search has been cut back to the kind of level you'd lay on for—for a stolen *car*, damn it! They've sent the army home; there's going to be an inquiry—Christ, it makes me sick. The pompous, block-headed, nit-witted old idiot!"

"But they mustn't!" Innis exclaimed. "We've had a casualty this morning—one of our staff came in without being told what was locked up in the constant-temperature room, and . . ." His voice trailed away.

"Has anyone else been reported missing yet?" Netta cried.

"That's the whole bloody point, isn't it?" Neville said savagely. "Someone gone missing the old fool might understand, but there just isn't room in his head for the idea of there being *too many* people! He thinks I'm crazy. And in the meantime that monster can roam loose all over the county!"

XXVIII

SHORT-HANDED BECAUSE of Sellers's absence at the research station, Branksome stood behind the inquiry desk at Brindown police station sifting through the morning's mail. A discreet cough attracted his attention, and he looked up to see a very embarrassed young man in a quasi-police uniform standing before him.

"Ah—morning, sergeant," he said. "I suppose really I ought to report this to Coastley police instead of you, but—well," he concluded in a burst of frankness, "I haven't the face to, because I know 'em all along there!"

"What's happened?" Branksome sighed.

"Well, my name's Pete Morley, and I work for Contract Security, looking after the docks at Coastley. And—well, this probably sounds bloody stupid, but I've lost my dog!"

"What?"

"It's a fact. A bloody great Alsatian. Answers to the name of Ajax. I've had him for three years—trained him myself—and this is the first time he's given me a lick of trouble. And I've got to have him back, or I'm out of a job until I can train another. And he cost me thirty-five quid when he was a pup barely big enough to walk by himself."

It was a change from the events of the weekend, anyhow, Branksome thought as he hid a grin and reached for his pad of report forms.

"This is one of the worst days I've ever lived through," Tom sighed, glancing around him at the darkening sea. He made to cast off the launch's painter. Monsters or not, the data gathered on their twice-daily trips had to be kept flowing, and that meant he and Netta had to go get it. Innis had been away since lunch-time on a series of frantic attempts to convince, if not the Chief Constable, then—or so he swore—the Prime Minister that the monster at large must be caught, and quickly.

Or rather, by now: *monsters*.

Sitting in the stern of the launch, Netta glanced at Inkosi hopefully wagging his tail on the wharf. She said, "Can't we take him with us for once?"

"Why not?" Tom shrugged. "No Sam Fletcher to complain, is there? Not now!"

"Tom—!"

"Please, love, don't tell me I'm being flippant when he's only been dead a few hours." Tom beckoned to the disbelieving dog who, convinced at last that he was invited along, jumped down and made the launch rock as he landed. "I'm more surprised than anything else at the luck we've had—and I do *not* mean luck in the sense that we lost Sam and not somebody else! I mean—well, suppose Bruno and his friends hadn't been on the beach when the creature came ashore: who would ever have noticed Miss Beeding's absence? The thing could have doubled itself half a dozen times over by now. Instead of which a sample was brought here within a matter of days, and we're on the way to understanding how to cope with it."

"Are we?" Netta sighed as she guided the launch out to sea. Nightfall had brought a cool breeze, but that wasn't why she shivered. "I can't help wondering if there is any way to deal with it. While you and Rory were trying to catch the two in the dolphin pen, he must have stuck his with his harpoon a dozen times. Yet there wasn't a mark on it when we dragged it ashore. It can repair its own damage at will, and that probably includes bullet-holes!"

"There'll be something that can stop it. There's bound to be." Tom spoke with more confidence than he felt. "A spray of acid, maybe. Or a flamethrower."

There was a pause. Netta said suddenly, "Wasn't it awful about that reporter?"

"Yes. I was sort of sorry for him. I always had the impression he wanted to be a nice person and simply didn't know how."

"Why do you think he did it?"

"I think it was Rory's fault."

"What? Talking to the reporter who got the garbled version into this morning's paper?"

"Doesn't that fit? Missing the chance to launch the biggest story of his career out of a fit of—of altruism?" Tom snorted. "Small wonder human beings don't go in for virtues much, if that's the reward they reap."

After that there was silence until they reached the first map reference where they had to take water samples. Inkosi, overjoyed to be with his owners, but sensing their depression, laid his chin on the gunwale and stared out to sea as though wondering why human beings behaved in this unaccountable manner. He was perfectly happy—why weren't they?

Driving homeward in the gathering dark, Branksome spared a hand from the wheel to rub his eyes tiredly. He had had a terrible day. Neville was furious at the Chief Constable's obtuseness, and had briefly visited his rage on Branksome. He'd apologized afterward, but it always made Branksome uncomfortable when one of his superiors lost enough self-control to take it out on his juniors. Meantime, whatever the Chief Constable might think after having Innis on his back—and according to an afternoon phone call, perhaps the Home Secretary by now if Innis had gone where he promised to go—he himself was convinced that there was at least a dangerous man in his area, liable to kill or maim, even if there wasn't the actual monstrous being the scientists at the research station were talking about.

He braked abruptly. In his headlights another car had appeared, half blocking the road, and its own lights showed a man bending over the body of a dog: an exceptionally big Alsatian. He suddenly remembered the shamefaced security guard who had come in this morning to report the loss of his dog, and pulled over.

It was not until he got out that he saw clearly what the other man was doing. He was holding a sharp, bright knife and slashing at the dead dog's belly.

"What are you doing?" Branksome demanded, striding forward.

The man raised his head. "Oh—oh, hello, sergeant. I've killed this beast, I'm afraid. Ran over it. I'm on my way home from delivering a premature baby. I'm a bit tired—didn't see it coming at me from the hedge."

"You're a doctor?" Branksome snapped; then, as the man's face showed, added, "Of course, I'm sorry. Dr.—Dr. Smith?"

"That's right."

"But what are you doing carving it up, for heaven's sake?"

Dr. Smith looked in embarrassment at the knife he held. He said, "Well, sergeant, it's—it's not a dog. It looks like a dog, but it isn't one. My bumper cut its belly open and all its guts spilled out, and that was about the first thing I noticed when I turned around and went back to look at what I'd run into."

"Not a dog?" Branksome echoed stupidly.

"Sounds damned silly, doesn't it? But I'd stake my

professional reputation on it. Did you ever hear of a dog with a vermiform appendix? Only human beings and sheep have them!"

A terrifying pattern of facts clicked together in Branksome's mind. He remembered as vividly as though he were in the room again the discussion between the scientists at the research station as they tried to explain why the specimen they were dissecting could be neither fish nor mammal.

He said faintly, "Then if it's not a dog . . ."

"Let's take a stroll on shore before we go back, shall we?" Netta proposed as she crated the last sample of water. "I'm sure Inkosi would approve." She rubbed the Ridgeback's head affectionately as he started up on hearing his name.

"Good idea," Tom said. "I'm much too worried to sleep, anyway, though after the last couple of days I ought to be dead beat. We can put into that beach there, can't we?"

Netta put the boat about. It was very late; the lights were going out in Coastley and Brindown both, meaning that midnight was past. Everything was very quiet.

"We should have done this tour the other way around," Tom said. "The Coastley side isn't nearly as nice as the Geddesley side, is it?"

"I'm glad we didn't," Netta said. "We'd probably have gone ashore somewhere near Miss Beeding's house."

The boat grounded. Tom helped Netta ashore and moored the launch to a tree root exposed by erosion. Inkosi, tail wagging like a mad semaphore flag, needed neither help nor encouragement. Arm in arm, silently, they walked along for two or three hundred yards while the dog pranced around them, leaving tokens of his visit.

Suddenly, however, he stopped dead and his spinal

ridge stood up vertically. He began to growl deep in his throat.

"Inkosi, what is it?" Netta demanded, and interrupted herself with a chuckle. "Oh, I get it! See him, Tom? Poor Inkosi must be jealous. Isn't he a beauty?"

Rising to all fours from a clump of grass ahead was a magnificent Alsatian.

"He's the biggest I've ever seen," Tom said. "I wonder if he's friendly. Here, boy!" He walked forward, holding out his hand. Instantly Inkosi leapt to place himself between his master and the Alsatian, crouching as though about to drive Tom bodily away.

"What on earth's got into you?" Tom exclaimed. "You are jealous, aren't you? Inkosi! Bad dog! Quiet!"

"Look out!" Netta shouted, and Inkosi reacted faster than Tom did. The Alsatian had suddenly charged, fangs bared, as though to sink them in the Ridgeback's nape, but Inkosi rolled aside and snapped upward with his own enormous jaws, ripping a gash in the Alsatian's throat. It howled and turned tail, and for all Netta and Tom's orders to return, Inkosi took out after it and vanished into the darkness, barking.

XXIX

WRAPPED IN A big sheet of polyethylene, the carcass of the dog-which-wasn't lay on the inquiry desk at the Brindown police station. Red-eyed with fatigue, Branksome sat waiting for Neville to turn up. The chief inspector hadn't welcomed being woken up, but as he'd said, with bitter irony, at least the new development meant that he had a new excuse for mounting a search, and a cordon around the area. A mad dog was something his superiors might have heard about.

The phone rang. He reached for it. "Brindown police— oh, yes, Dr. Reedwall? . . . Your dog? Got in a fight with an Alsatian?"

"It wasn't much of a fight," Tom said, sounding embarrassed. "But he drew enough blood for us to follow the trail for quite some distance. Then we lost it on the outskirts of Coastley. And my wife's dreadfully tired, so . . . But if anyone sees a Ridgeback wandering around—"

"It sounds as though you've had a very narrow escape, sir," Branksome said with a shiver.

"What?"

"We've found out how the monster eluded our search. It's taken over the shape of a dog this time. A doctor ran over one of them and spotted that the internal organs weren't right."

"A dog!" Tom whistled. "Then Inkosi must have scented there was something wrong, and . . . But that's a brilliant idea! What better disguise for it among human beings? Are you going to look for it?"

"I'm waiting for Chief Inspector Neville now."

"Well, look, I've got something you may find useful. I'll bring it over. Where will you be?"

"I suppose we'll start looking where— Hang on." The other phone was ringing, and Branksome seized it. "Yes?"

"Neville," it said. "I'm going straight to the docks. Meet me there. County HQ put out an all-cars just now reporting a disturbance. The security officer says he was attacked by a mad dog. Sounds like ours—hurry!"

At the gate of the small Coastley docks, an ambulance had already arrived. In its headlights, the security officer Branksome had met before—Pete Morley—was having his hand dressed in bandages. Neville was talking urgently with Sellers, who looked half-dead with weariness and very resentful at being called out yet again.

Branksome approached Morley and greeted him. He added in a low voice, "Was it your own dog that did this to you?"

"I *thought* it was Ajax," Morley said in a depressed tone. "Called him, he didn't come, and when I went after him . . ."

He shrugged, as though the world had become too complicated for him to cope with.

"Sergeant!" Neville said, coming over. Behind him Branksome saw Sellers hurrying toward a phone booth at the corner of the street. "I've sent Sellers to call the fire brigade, and we'll wait until they get here, I think."

"Uh—why?" Branksome said, wondering if fatigue had made him stupid.

"Told them to bring along protective clothing. Fire-fighting suits. And maybe a weapon, too. I put my shotgun in the car, but unless I'm badly mistaken no guns will harm one of these shapechangers. On the other hand—well, did you ever see a man hit by a hundred-pound jet of water?" He added dryly, "And since the Chief Constable objected to my asking for help from the army—well, I've got to get men from somewhere. Ah, here's the answer to our all-cars!"

A car came swerving toward them, braking as it drew level, but it wasn't a police car, as they realized when the lights went out. From it jumped Tom Reedwall, carrying a curious makeshift device consisting of a cylinder mounted on a rough wooden stock and a sort of pump with a cross-handle. He recognized them and called out, but as he came toward them the first of the police cars appeared in response to the radio message, and Neville strode off to brief the occupants.

"What's that you've got?" Branksome asked Tom.

"I made it out of one of my scuba air tanks and a lab pump," Tom said. "It's got about three pints of pure nitric acid in it. I can't imagine anything else doing much harm to this damned beast, and this is all we had at the labs. But it might help, I guess."

The fire engine roared up before Branksome could comment, and several puzzled men got down from it, dutifully carrying protective suits of aluminized heat-proof fabric, with helmets and gauntlets to match. Neville called them over to him, and everyone else except the ambulance men attending to Morley went close.

"We don't know exactly what we've got here," Neville said loudly. "We think probably a mad dog that has been smuggled in without going through quarantine. We're going to surround the interior of the wire fence that encloses the docks, and work inward. We're also going to close in the seaward side, because we daren't let the beast get to the water. That's assuming it hasn't escaped that way already. Before you say anything: no, dogs with hydrophobia are *not* terrified by the sight of water. Any questions?"

One of the firemen said, "We need guns for this job, don't we?"

"A shotgun is available and I'll bring it with me. But you brought the equivalent of a gun with you. Run out your hoses and deploy them around the area. And let's have those protective suits."

Tom said, "Chief Inspector!"

"Yes?"

"There may be two dogs here. Mine apparently—uh—saved my life, Sergeant Branksome says. Must have smelled something bad about this one we're after. He may have managed to bay it, the way his breed do with lions in Africa. I—uh—I wouldn't want to lose him."

"What color is yours?"

"Brown. The other one is black, the one we want."

"Everyone hear that? Right, issue the protective suits."

Explaining to Neville about his improvised acid-gun had secured Tom one of the fire-fighting suits. Feeling very clumsy and vulnerable in it, holding his peculiar weapon at waist height, he stood beside the gates to the dock area as they were opened to admit first the police cars, which roared off in opposite directions to take up station at equally spaced points around the perimeter, then the fire engines—by now, there were three of them—to search for hydrants and connect their hoses.

Then Neville, recognizable only by his voice because he too had put on one of the protective suits, ordered his own party to start their methodical survey of the mazelike docks.

By night, this was an eerie and confusing area. There were few lights, and those high overhead on cables strung between tall poles. Piled crates with tarpaulins over them

211

took on the outlines of weather-beaten rocks; hawsers in coils lay like the casts of some colossal worm. Every time the sea breeze made one of the lamps swing, it altered the relation of light to dark on the ground below, giving the illusion of a slow ocean swell, as though the concrete they walked across were changed to a dense, tarry liquid in a rocking bowl.

In a little while, the firemen had rigged their iodine-quartz spotlights and shot spears of diamond brilliance across the docks. But that was at best of temporary help. At first they were moving among low stacks of goods, grouped barrels, cardboard packages protected from the risk of rain with polyethylene sheets, and suchlike obstructions over the tops of which they could see one another. A few yards on, however, they reached a section where apparently a whole ship's cargo had been newly discharged and crammed into the smallest possible area. A crane like a colossal mantis stooped over wooden crates, bales, and packages heaped thirty, forty, fifty feet high in irregular close-set stacks like the stepped relic of a lava flow, a miniature Giant's Causeway.

Tom was about to enter a narrow alley leading between two high stacks of crates when Neville shouted at him.

"Don't go down any passages like that! Go over the top and look down—use your torch!"

Alarmed, Tom saw the good sense of the advice, and realized that there were ladders propped here and there against the sides of the stacked crates and bales, presumably for the men who guided the crane's loads into position. He made for the nearest, swinging his torch along the shadowed base of the stack, and suddenly stopped dead.

In the circle of light: a brown tail, not moving.

"Inkosi!" he breathed, and the tail gave a trembling acknowledgment.

"Here!" Tom shouted, and Neville came hurrying over

as he bent to examine the dog in the light of the torch. All Inkosi's nape and shoulders were matted with blood, and one of his hind legs was so tender he yelped when it was touched, but he seemed mainly exhausted; after a few moments he was able to try and stand up, though his injured leg betrayed him.

"Think the—the monster is up there?" Neville whispered, as though afraid of being overheard, and gestured toward the high irregular face of the stacked crates.

"If Inkosi could move at all, he'd follow what he was after," Tom said positively. "I'd lay a bet—yes! Look out!"

He jumped back, torch jerking up to outline what he had seen silhouetted against the sky: devil-savage, a thing neither canine nor human, with sharp nose, gaping jaws, and—

"God, it's got *hands*!" Neville exclaimed.

"It—it can change deliberately if it has to," Tom said, struggling to be rational in face of this unprecedented menace. "We saw on Rory Dunstable's film. . . . What the—?"

Something slammed down from overhead, almost unseen because of his helmet, and struck his shoulder a painful blow.

"That's why it gave itself hands! To climb ladders, and to throw things!" he exclaimed. "I'll guard this side, sir—I don't think it can get past me. Call the others in!"

But at the same moment one of the swiveling spotlights chanced in this direction, and the creature was brilliantly lit for the world to see. Hairy-headed, obscenely naked where it had chosen to make itself over and regain the power to clutch and throw, it ducked down between two crates and howled.

"After it!" Neville snapped, cradling his gun under one arm and scrambling up the ladder.

"With you in a moment, boy," Tom whispered to Inkosi, and followed him.

They were not the only men to make the ascent. As soon as Tom put his head over the side of the stack, he noticed that four or more of the other searchers had found ladders and been able to get up here before him. Torches and clubs in hand, they stood on the edge of the stack and stared. In the middle of the ring, the monster half-stood, half-crouched, as though not only its body but its mind were confused between canine and human.

Pace by pace, the men closed in. There was a good distance to cover because this was by far the largest stack of goods in the dockyard. Snarling, the monster scrabbled at the surface it stood on—

And snapped into motion faster than the eye could follow! It had torn up the lid of the crate beneath its feet with more than human strength, and hurled the whole of it—a four-foot square of nailed boards—at the two men opposite Tom. It caught them with its corners and spun them around; one stumbled back and toppled over the edge of the stack with a scream.

Out of the open crate the monster clawed something else and threw that—Tom couldn't see what, but the force behind the impact was like a boxer's punch, and the third man fell. The survivor turned and climbed to a higher level, but as he clambered up the monster raised its arm again.

And Neville let his shotgun go, both barrels in a single coughing roar.

The creature howled, and spun around, and threw at him instead of its original target, and the missile struck Neville's helmet at forehead height. He cried out, threw up both arms in spasm, and let the gun fall.

And the creature, having absorbed the full charge from both cartridges, bared its teeth and leapt at Tom.

Wildly he pumped the handle of his improvised spray-gun. A mist of acid sprang from the nozzle of the cylinder. The creature met it in midspring and howled again, falling to one side of him, clawing at its eyes with both hands. Desperately, he kept on pumping, seeing the flesh writhe under the acid, keeping after the beast as it frog-hopped sidelong toward the open crate and the source of the missiles that had rid it of four of its hunters.

Tom came after, prodigally spending the acid until brown smoking smears appeared on the crates. The monster reached its goal, its flesh running almost liquidly now, its eyes bulbing out above its ruined cheeks as though it were concentrating all its ability to mend its injuries on those essential guides to the world. It clutched something from the crate, and the same instant the spray-gun uttered its last dribble of acid.

Tom raised it feebly before him as though he could hope to ward off the monster's attack with it, half-seeing from the corner of his eye how Neville was wavering dazedly to his feet—and the world seemed to explode.

Under the monster, from the open crate, a sudden roaring flame shot up, and a cloud of choking smoke amid which the beast vanished, howling again like a lost soul hurled into the pit of hell. Staring incredulously, Tom saw by the light of the incomprehensible blaze something he had not noticed before: on every crate, a label in warning red.

Danger—Flammable—Pyrotechnic Goods.

He laughed insanely and turned to help Neville toward the ladder and the safety of the ground. He guided the policeman over it, assisted him in finding purchase for his feet, and—

"Reedwall! Look out!" Neville shouted as he turned at the top of the ladder. Tom spun on his heel. There, coming out of the welling smoke, was the monster again, arms up like a bear to hug and kill, only two yards from him!

"Jump!" Neville shouted, and did so himself, vanishing as though he had dematerialized. Tom tried to copy him, but a touch came on his shoulder as the monster lunged, took a grip—

And was bowled back, hurled off its feet, sent sprawling into the heart of the now raging blaze, by the white lance of water from a fire hose.

It gave one last scream of mortal agony, and then the world was instantly quiet, except for the licking crackle of the flames and the soft inquiring whimper from below which meant that Inkosi wanted to know if he was all right.

Slowly, his limbs like lead after that narrow escape, Tom found footholds on the ladder and made his way to the ground.

XXX

BRUNO BACKED THE van into what he had now come to think of as its usual parking space beside the gate of the marine research station, and switched off. He and Cress got down and walked hand in hand toward the buildings.

"It's very quiet," Cress said as they approached. "It is a weekday, isn't it? I get mixed up sometimes."

"Somebody must be about," Bruno shrugged, and called out. In answer, there was a knocking noise, and a large brown shape emerged hobbling and heavily smeared around the neck with white ointment, from behind the corner of the main labs. It was his tail banging the wall that signaled his presence.

"Goodness, Inkosi! You have been in the wars, haven't you?" Cress said, bending down to pat the uninjured area of his back.

"There they are—Tom and Netta, and Dr. Innis," Bruno said, and added, "They look terrible! Christ, has something else gone wrong now? I thought it was all over."

Diffidently they approached the three scientists and received nods of greeting.

"What's happened?" Cress demanded.

"I'm sorry if we appear uncivil," Innis said, passing his hand through his white hair. "We've just been witnesses at a rather disgusting spectacle. The—ah—the demise of the two surviving shapechangers."

"When they didn't manage to get out and attack fresh

217

prey," Netta amplified, "they—well, they just turned on each other and tore themselves into bits. I never saw anything so revolting."

"It was to be expected," Tom muttered, taking out his pipe and filling it absently. "It must require a hell of a lot of energy to undergo that change process. No wonder they have to feed every couple of days."

"You mean the things never eat except when they—?" Cress hesitated, at a loss for the right word.

"Yes, as far as we can make out from the paucity of specimen material remaining to us, they merely copy and don't utilize the digestive organs of their prey. As the time for feeding and changing approaches, their entire abdominal protoplasm deliquesces into that extraordinary acid that cost our Irish friend his hand when it was sucked in through the creature's integument. Amazing creatures!" Innis shook his head in wonderment, then briskened.

"And what can we do for you this fine day?"

"Well, we just drove over to see how things were here," Bruno said. "We're working at the holiday camp near Coastley the whole of next week, and I had to come down today and finalize the arrangements. Big scene, lots of money. A pretty square crowd, of course, but the manager doesn't know anything about the music so he's giving us our heads to do what we like, and I guess we'll make out okay."

"Are you going to hold the—what do you call it?—the freakout on the beach you came down to arrange in the first place?" Tom inquired.

"Not in *that* place," Cress said firmly. "But we're going to have a beach party at the camp if the weather's fine."

"Big finale at the end of our stay," Bruno said. "A week Saturday. Rupert's there at the moment. He does all our special sonic effects and he's working up a grand design for the whole thing." He hesitated. "I—uh—I was going to ask if you'd like some tickets."

"Sure, we'd love to come," Tom said, and Netta nodded.

"How about you, Dr. Innis?"

Innis's eyes twinkled. "I think I'm probably a bit past it by now, young fellow. And yet . . . Well, damn it, yes, I will, and thank you. I'll at least drop by and see if it cheers me up. I shall need it by next Saturday, I'm sure of that."

As they talked, they had been walking slowly between the buildings, and now came in sight of the Reedwalls' bungalow. "Come in and have a beer," Tom suggested. "I don't think I'm fit to go straight back to work after what we've been seeing."

There was a moment of silence. Then Cress said, "Why will you need cheering up so much, Dr. Innis?"

Innis sighed. "This thing isn't over by a very long chalk, young lady! You've no idea what a mass of bureaucratic inertia we've set ponderously rolling down the various 'official channels'!" He made the phrase sound almost obscene, and went on as Tom ushered them into the house, "Just to begin with, our late unfortunate colleague. There must be an inquest, naturally, and in addition our employers the government want to know where one of their staff went to without leaving the customary—ah—remains. I hope I don't sound excessively cynical; it's merely that I'm steeling myself for the official inquiry, which begins on Monday with the descent of various senior scientific officers from Whitehall, none of whom have actually done any work in their alleged speciality for a good decade or more. . . . Ah, thank you!" He accepted the beer Netta offered and took a healthy swig of it.

"As a matter of fact, it's not beyond the bounds of possibility that your band may be called to give evidence, but we'll avoid that if we can, naturally—don't want to inconvenience you.

"And over and above that—well, there's the unfortunate plight of Chief Inspector Neville. I didn't like him when I first met him, but he certainly knew the truth when he saw it and acted accordingly. But for his willingness to risk the wrath of his superiors, I think the shapechanger might easily have got away in its dog's guise. It was an inspiration, if it was a deliberate choice. That, though, we shall never know."

"But that's not the half of it," Tom said. "I was talking to Sergeant Branksome yesterday. Apparently there's a police board of inquiry due to be held, too, to establish why Neville called out the army to look for a hypothetical lunatic, and why he caused the destruction of three thousand pounds' worth of marine signal flares at Coastley docks. They didn't actually go off, of course, or I wouldn't be here—I was standing right on top of them. But the firemen doused the entire consignment and ruined the lot." He paused, eyeing Bruno and Cress.

"You—ah—you do know about this, do you?" he said.

"Some of it," Bruno nodded. "We sort of pieced it together from what there was in the papers. But all the news stories were scrappy; it didn't look as though anyone fitted the whole lot together."

"That is something to be thankful for," Innis said. "But don't make the mistake of imagining that the problem isn't being taken seriously, will you? I sent that film of Mr. Dunstable's to a friend of mine who specializes in the unmasking of forgeries, and he's told me on the phone that he's prepared to certify to its being neither faked nor tampered with. I have consequently managed to spread a little alarm and despondency in official circles, and I foresee a campaign somewhat similar to the Colorado beetle one, warning fishermen to be wary of certain types of catch."

"You mean there—" Cress's face fell. "Of course! I'd completely forgotten that there must be others, out there in the sea. Christ, I'll never dare to go for a swim again!" She jerked forward on her chair. "But why haven't you warned everybody? It could attack someone tomorrow!"

"We think not," Netta said reassuringly. "We've had time to study the complete specimen Mr. Fleet brought us from the Organic Acids depot, and—well, I won't go into the technical details, but it looks as though this is definitely a deep-water fish. We found some compounds in its protoplasm which have only previously been identified in fish from below five hundred fathoms. We think ours was a stray that normally feeds on the giant squids, and wandered out of its normal habitat—got lost, in fact. You saw in Rory's film how the one he caught tried to change into a squid form when it was in danger, didn't you? When it came into shallow water, it must have had difficulty finding adequate food—the fish simply weren't big enough. And as we saw this morning, when it doesn't get the food it needs, it . . ." She swallowed hard and sipped her beer, shrugging.

"Which was why it chose the body of the pilot instead of another fish?" Bruno suggested.

"Precisely," Tom agreed. "Lord, I'm glad to know the other ones, still out there in the sea, are probably starving! Think what a lot of damage just one of them did when it acquired access to human memory and intelligence! Poor old Miss Beeding—the nurse at the mental hospital—Sam Fletcher!"

"And the reporter," Cress said. "In a way."

"Yes, of course. Poor devil."

There was a pause. Tom broke it, rising to his feet.

"Well, we've got to sort of batten down the hatches here before the inquiry descends on us next Monday, so we'd better make a move."

"Thanks for the beer," Bruno said, and with Cress beside him headed for the door. On the threshold he checked and glanced back, through the window overlooking the sea.

"Do you people really know what goes on out there?" he said.

"We know a little," Innis said. "We suspect more. But that's the most we can claim."

Bruno nodded. "We took the octopus off the van," he said. "I don't think any of us will ever be able to make another joke about the sea or what comes out of it. . . . Well, thanks again, and we'll see you next Saturday."

He took Cress's hand, and together they walked into the sunshine.

DEL REY SCIENCE FICTION CLASSICS
FROM BALLANTINE BOOKS

CHILDHOOD'S END, Arthur C. Clarke	27603	1.95
FAHRENHEIT 451, Ray Bradbury	27431	1.95
HAVE SPACESUIT, WILL TRAVEL, Robert A. Heinlein	26071	1.75
IMPERIAL EARTH, Arthur C. Clarke	25352	1.95
MORE THAN HUMAN, Theodore Sturgeon	24389	1.50
RENDEZVOUS WITH RAMA, Arthur C. Clarke	27344	1.95
RINGWORLD, Larry Niven	27550	1.95
A SCANNER DARKLY, Philip K. Dick	26064	1.95
SPLINTER OF THE MIND'S EYE, Alan Dean Foster	26062	1.95
STAND ON ZANZIBAR, John Brunner	25486	1.95
STAR WARS, George Lucas	26079	1.95
STARMAN JONES, Robert A. Heinlein	27595	1.75
TUNNEL IN THE SKY, Robert A. Heinlein	26065	1.50
UNDER PRESSURE, Frank Herbert	27540	1.75